A Barrel of Laughs, A Vale of Tears

♦

JULES FEIFFER

A Barrel of Laughs, A Vale of Tears

Michael di Capua Books ♦ HarperCollins Publishers

Library of Congress catalog card number: 94-79737

Printed in the United States of America

Designed by Steve Scott

First edition, 1995

First paperback edition, 1998

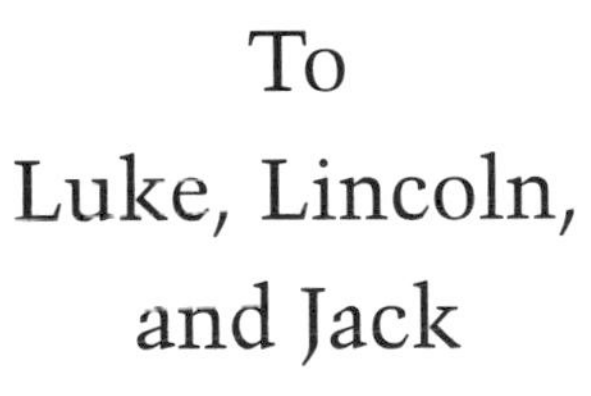

To
Luke, Lincoln,
and Jack

Contents

♦

A Barrel of Laughs,
A Vale of Tears

♦

Chapter 1

The Hunter of Boar or Stag

Roger

had a strange effect on people.

Take this guy. See how grumpy he is?

He's been grumpy since he got out of bed, stepped on his little boy's beach ball, slid halfway across the house, and flew out the window into the rosebush. Wouldn't you be grumpy with a dozen thorns in your head?

Don't get too interested in this character. He's in our story just as an example and we'll leave him forever in nine pages.

Now here is our guy trekking through the forest, hunting boar or hunting stag—something like that—because that's what men did in Roger's day. They got up in the morning and said, "Wife, I am going out to hunt," and Wife said, "What will you bring home today, Husband, boar or stag?" And the man of the house would reply, "Whatever," because it really didn't matter: all food tasted the same (not too good) in those days. Ketchup hadn't been invented.

So he's trekking through the woods—trek, trek, trek—a big frown on his face because he's thinking: "Why does everything happen to me? First I trip on my kid's ball, get a crownful of thorns, stub my toe on the doorsill, get laughed at by my wife who calls me a clumsy oaf, which I am, but if she truly loved me she wouldn't say so. I hate my wife—er—that is, my life. I also hate hunting boar or stag. I should have been a blacksmith. Thank the Lord that in eight more pages I'll be out of this book forever!"

He's thinking all this garbage
when, for no reason at all,
the frown leaves his face.

He treks another five yards and,
for no reason at all, he smiles.

He treks still another five yards and,
for no reason at all, he grins from ear to ear.

And he feels wonderful, better than he has since he won last year's sack race at the Peasants' Picnic.

Now, although I've written "for no reason at all"—and repeated it twice—there *was* a reason. The hunter didn't realize that Roger was trekking toward him from the opposite direction.

And the closer Roger got to him, the more cheerful the hunter became. *That* was the effect Roger had on people. He made them feel good.

He didn't do anything to make them feel good. He didn't tell jokes. He didn't try to please—he didn't have to: he was a prince.

Roger was the son of kindly King Whatchamacallit. And, being a prince, he had the right to be stern, haughty, and bad-tempered. Except he couldn't be, because he didn't know what it was to be stern, haughty, or bad-tempered. He had never seen any examples. He had never seen his father, the king, throw a fit, or his dear departed mother, the queen, stamp her foot in anger. Nor had he seen out of sorts any of the king's ministers, courtiers, chefs, servants, maids, or lackeys. Not once since his birth had he heard an angry scream, shout, curse, or quarrel. Not once had he seen a tear, unless it was tears of joy. And of those he saw many.

Because Roger was a carrier of joy, he spread it before him. It glowed off his presence like the rays of the sun. He was a special delight to his mother, and the thought of this he found particularly gratifying because of her sudden demise. Out for a swim one day, she'd been swallowed by a blue whale.

He missed his mother, but whales were his favorite mammal and blue was his favorite color, so, if she had to go, that didn't seem like such a bad way. After a while, Roger came to smile at the thought of that blue whale on that bright green sea gulping down his mother in a red-striped swimming costume as if she was a candy cane.

Everything in life amused Roger. Here he is waking up in the morning.

This is the morning he planned to go horseback riding on the royal grounds. But it's a terrible day. It's raining. Not only is it raining, it's sleeting and hailing at the same time. Hailstones, sounding like gunshots, bounce off the palace walls. So what does Roger say to himself as he looks out the window? He says: "Wow! I'll get drenched to my loincloth in two seconds flat if I go out in this. I can't wait!"

He doesn't go back to bed and read a royal book or magazine as any prince in his right mind might do. He goes out and gets soaked and slapped around by hailstones and—if you can believe it—he has a good time.

Everything, significant or insignificant, gave Roger a good time. Brushing his teeth gave him a good time. Eating and sleeping gave him a good time. Sport amused him: hunting, archery, jousting. Kindness amused him, but no more than cruelty. Fat people, skinny people, rich people, poor people, vagrants, all caused him to giggle. People who lived in castles with dozens of servants they couldn't keep track of, this gave him a good laugh.

Roger's remarkably high spirits cast a spell over anyone or anything who came within a half mile of him.

Dogs ceased chasing cats.

Cats quit chasing birds.

Birds were charmed out of the trees
and stopped hunting worms.

Worms curled and uncurled in spasms of glee.

And laughing hyenas laughed so extra-hard they had to stuff their mouths with dead branches and foul-tasting foliage in order to regain their composure.

By now, you get the picture. And here's our friend, the hunter, back in the picture.

Roger has just come into view and the hunter has collapsed, screaming with laughter. Oops, he's collapsed into another rosebush.

He's too busy laughing to know how awful he's going to feel in a minute. But that's all right, because as of this moment he's out of the book. He was here just to show us the effect Roger has on people.

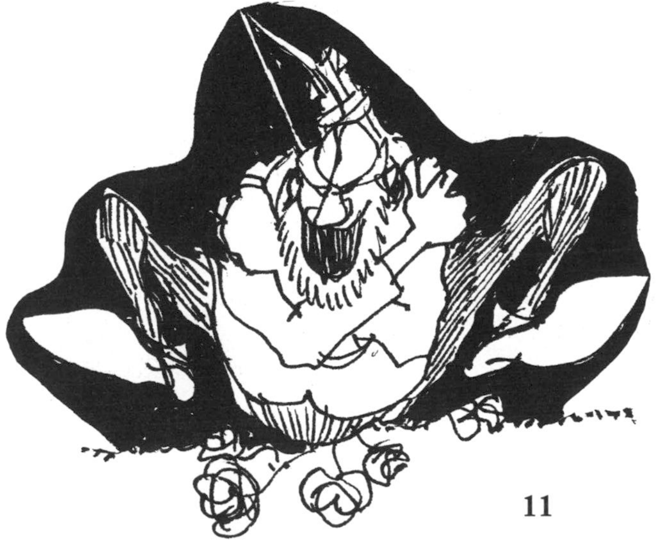

Mr. Hunter,
you can go now.

He's still laughing.

Sir, it's time for you to leave.

He's not leaving. He's still laughing.
He won't leave.

I hate to lose control of a book this way.
Okay, so *we'll* leave and go on to the next chapter.

Chapter 2

King Whatchamacallit

"Roger, this can go not on," said his father, the king, from the throne room of his castle.

Roger was not present when the king spoke. If he had been, the king would not have been able to get much more than a word or two out, like: "Roger, this—this—*ha-ha*—this—this—this—*ha-ha-ha-ha-ha-ha-ha-ha-ha-ha-ha-ha*—" and so on, till he died of laughter or old age.

Father and son spoke to each other on the "thingamajibbet," which is what the king, who didn't know the right word for anything, called his wizard's invention, which was two paper cups connected by a string five miles long. It stretched from the king's throne room out the castle window over hill and dale, forest and field, river and mountain, to the highest peak in the kingdom, where there stood a tower built for Roger alone, the one place on earth he could hang out without causing laughter.

"Roger, I kiss you merry such, I mean I miss you very much, but when you're around no done gets work, I mean no work gets done, because bodyevery's laughing." The king knew what he meant, but it took him more than one try to say it, and that's why he came to be called King Whatchamacallit.

"My son, when you're around, no till gets soiled—er, no soil gets tilled, no noo gets shaled—that is, no shoe gets nailed, no bag gets stagged—I mean, no stag gets bagged. And I'll bell you fie, sell you tie, tell you why.

"Because you're too darn likable. Hmm, is that right?" It confused the king when he spoke correctly. "I'll be king someday—that is, *you'll* king be someday, and that's laughing to noth at—er, nothing to laugh at. A laugh is no kinging matter—that is, a king is no laughing hatter—laughing matter. Someplace you'll be in my day—er, someday you'll be in my place and you'll want—you'll demand—you'll demand—what is that word? Collect, dissect, insect, *respect*! Word the that's! Respect! Yes! But not if you're a staffinglock, laughingstock. Roger, it's time you did something with myself—yourself. You need a cooler and wiser sled, bed—that is, head. I'm sending see to you my gizzard, lizard, blizzard, *wizard*!"

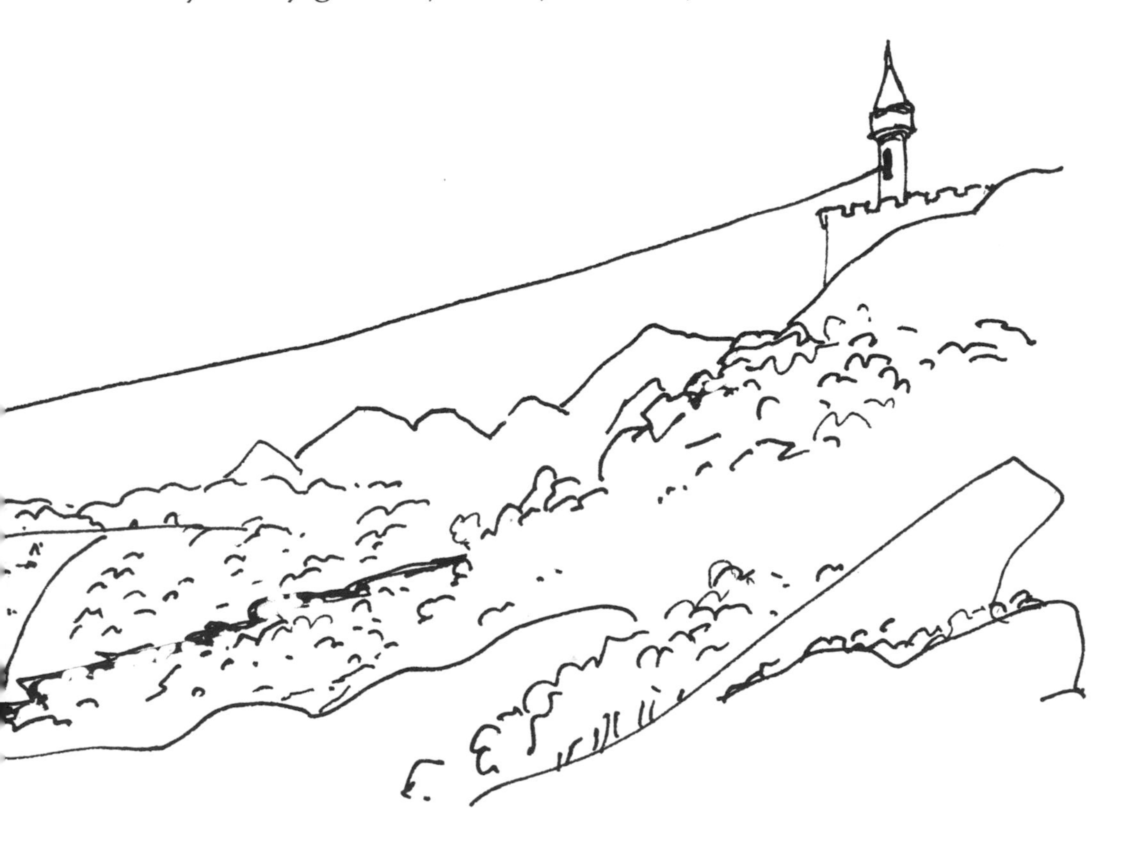

Chapter 3

J. Wellington Wizard

Where is Roger in this picture?

__ A. Behind the drapes

__ B. Under the chair

__ C. Under the man's robes

__ D. Not in this picture

__ E. Other

E is correct. The old, beat-up, lumpy armchair in which the old, beat-up, lumpy man is sitting is—guess who?—Roger! He is being sat on by J. Wellington Wizard, who was not only the wisest man in the kingdom but also a great magician. But as wise and great as J. Wellington was, he could not be in Roger's company without rolling around on the floor, helpless with laughter. And this was undignified for a man of his position, and dangerous for a man of his age, which was 132.

The only way J. Wellington could be around Roger without rolling on the floor was to cast a spell which turned the boy into something that wasn't likely to make him laugh. At one time or another, he had turned Roger into a dog, a cat, a mouse, a frog, a tree, a raindrop, a ball of dust. But on this day, because he was exhausted, having been up all night writing predictions for the coming century, he decided to kill two birds with one stone and turn Roger into an armchair.

"Am I too heavy for you, Roger?"

"No, sir. Ha-ha."

"Did I say something funny?"

"Not yet, but I'm getting ready. Ha-ha."

"Let me place a stuffed pillow on your seat and see if that quiets you down. Do you mind?"

"No problem, ha-ha."

J. Wellington looked surprised, then he looked displeased. "Roger, I have been up all night transcribing predictions for the next century. And not even then will anyone have heard the phrase 'No problem.' 'No problem' will not become a figure of speech for—oh, I predict, another six hundred years. I hate it in books or movies or TV when people living in times like ours use language that won't be in use for centuries hence."

"What's movies? What's TV?"

"Forget it!" snapped the Wizard, uttering a phrase that wouldn't be used again for six centuries.

"Sorry about that," said Roger.

"Be my guest," said the Wizard.

"That's cool," said Roger.

"No problem," growled the Wizard, concluding the exchange, which hadn't gone at all as he intended.

And this was typical of Roger: Nothing went as it was supposed to.

"Roger," said J. Wellington, determined to make himself understood, "for everyone but you, life has its ups and downs, its sunshine and clouds."

"Incredible!" said Roger.

J. Wellington was astonished. "Ups and downs, sunshine and clouds sound incredible to you?"

"I couldn't wish for more," said the armchair who was Roger, "unless it's—hold on!—ins and outs, lights and darks, smooths and roughs, wins and losses, and—wait a minute, there's one more—one more—oh, yes—bitters and sweets. Can I have them, too?"

J. Wellington hunched his old, wizened, wizard's body and addressed the armchair sternly. "No, Roger. None of these can you have. Not now. Not ever. Do you want to know why?"

"This is hilarious," said the armchair.

"*That's* why!" snapped J. Wellington. "Because you are amused by everyone and you amuse everyone. Roger, you do not have a serious bone in your body. You have only funny bones. And a prince with no bones but funny bones is unprepared to be a king, a father—or even a grown-up. You are not ready, you may never be ready, to take on the duties, obligations, and responsibilities of your station."

"If this is my station, I'd better get off!" cracked Roger.

"There is a world out there, you popinjay!" roared J. Wellington in frustration. He pointed out the window toward the Forever Forest and beyond. "It is a mixed-up universe full of sun and shadow, highlights and lowlifes. And none of this will you experience. None of *anything* will you experience." J. Wellington rose from Roger and crossed over to the window. He stared out for a long time. "You have yet to venture on a quest," he said. A gleam was in his eye.

"A *what*?" asked Roger.

"Exactly!" cried the wizard. "The thing to do is send you on a quest!"

"Like rescuing a beautiful maiden from a dragon or an ogre? That could be good for a laugh!"

"Roger, you are far too light-headed for rescues. I can just imagine you on a steed charging to the rescue of a fair maiden held captive by a dragon . . ." The wizard could not help grinning at the thought. "The poor dragon!" He chuckled. "The pathetic maiden!" He giggled. "They would die—die—die—" He could not get the words out. "Die—die—die—die—die laugh—laugh—laughingggg!" He fell to the floor, helpless with glee, rolling this way and that. Not until he managed to sputter the words "Close, Sesame" was the old magician able to control himself. His lips clamped shut as if nailed. His color went from beet red to bread white. He glared at Roger as he rose—actually floated (because he was a magician)—to his feet.

"You see what you do, Roger? You put the entire kingdom into an uproar. We shall never have peace until you return from your quest a more levelheaded fellow."

"What quest?" asked Roger, just as J. Wellington sat back down on him.

"A quest that offers you more than mere adventure," mused J. Wellington. "A quest that offers you—" J. Wellington unfurled the next word like a flag: "Exxxperrrienccce!"

Roger was puzzled. "I think that's the longest word I have ever heard, except for 'hippopotamus.' What does it mean?"

"I'm your wizard, not your tutor. You will know soon enough what it means," grunted J. Wellington. "Shall I start you out on the Plain of Pain, which will lead you into the Chasm of Crisis, then end it all in the Den of Doom . . ." He shook his head. "No, that's far too advanced. You need a quest you can grow on."

"Isn't it a quest when you have to find something, or somebody?" said Roger.

"Exactly!" said the Wizard, delighted with Roger's grasp of the matter.

"Who or what do I have to find?"

"I'm glad you asked me that question," said J. Wellington. He rose from Roger and crossed to the window. His entire body ached from rolling this way and that on the

floor. He stared out the window with a magician's gaze, taking in forests, mountains, valleys that no ordinary eye could see.

"I see you entering the Forever Forest, Roger." J. Wellington spoke in a voice so low that Roger, the chair, had to strain to hear it.

"The Forever Forest, what's that?" asked Roger.

"Continuing on to the Dastardly Divide."

"The Dastardly Divide, what's that?" asked Roger.

"From there to the Valley of Vengeance."

"The Valley of Vengeance, what's that?" asked Roger.

"Across the Sea of Screams and the Mountain of Malice."

"Is that it? Or is there more?" asked Roger. "Because if there's more, I'd just as soon not know."

A cunning glint set off sparks in J. Wellington's eye. "There you shall find your quest!"

"I don't understand," said Roger. "Where?"

"Betwixt, between, or beyond," said the wizard.

"Let me see if I have this straight," said Roger. "I shall either find my quest in one of those places, or somewhere else. Is that what you're telling me?"

"Betwixt, between, or beyond," repeated the wizard.

Roger shook with laughter, which was a sight to see because he was a chair. "You're sending me off on a quest, you won't tell me where, to find you won't tell me what. Do I have that right?"

"I couldn't have said it better myself," said the wizard.

"Said what?" chuckled Roger. "I don't know what I said! How will I know that I'm at where I'm going? Or that I've found what I'm looking for?" Roger asked in a building, burbling laugh that went on for nearly a minute.

"That is how," grumbled J. Wellington Wizard.

"What is how?" giggled Roger, unable to contain himself.

"Wherever it is, whatever it is, whoever it is, you will know you have found it when neither of you is laughing."

"Whoopee!" cried Roger, rattling back and forth so hard that an armrest came loose and bounced across the floor, bashing J. Wellington in the ankle.

"Yeearghooowcheeackywow!" cried the wizard, using a word that had nothing to do with magic but described exactly the way he felt.

Chapter 4

The Forever Forest

After two days and nights of travel, Roger, who had been turned into a white horse, and J. Wellington Wizard, who rode him, arrived just after dawn at the entrance to the Forever Forest. "Looks perfectly pleasant to me," said Roger, observing trees of every shape and size swaying like dancers in the early-morning mist.

J. Wellington snapped his fingers one and a half times, which was exactly what he needed to do to turn Roger back into his prince of a self. Then the boy and the old wizard made their farewells.

As he tearfully embraced Roger, J. Wellington found that he still had to laugh. "Roger, *ha-ha* I give you this bag of Magic Powder that you must keep with you at all times. It will change you into things that amuse *ha-ha* no one. Precisely what and for how long I cannot *ha-ha* say. Magic is an inexact *ha-ha* science. You could be a squirrel *ha-ha* for an hour, a goose *ha-ha* for a day, a fern *ha-ha* for a week, a tree for a—for a—oh, *ha-ha-ha-ha-ha-ha*, I can't stand this! Good luck, my boy!"

Before Roger had a chance to share a last laugh with

him, J. Wellington pulled his black traveling cloak up over his peaked wizard's hat and spun away like a top.

Roger entered the Forever Forest, convinced that he could cheerfully dash through to the Dastardly Divide, the Valley of Vengeance, the Sea of Screams, the Mountain of Malice, and be back in his tower with the results of his quest (whatever it turned out to be) by nightfall.

A year later, he was still certain that it wouldn't take long. But the further he trekked—trek, trek, trek—the more lost he got. The Forever Forest started here but never got there, which is why it was called the Forever Forest. It went on and on and on and on and on some more. Roger ran into wanderers who had been in it for fifteen or twenty years. They didn't get to laugh at Roger, because at the sound of their approach (giggles followed by guffaws), he splashed himself with Magic Powder from the wizard's sack. And within the blink of an eye, he was transformed. Into all sorts of things; for example:

A daisy.

A cow.

A snake.

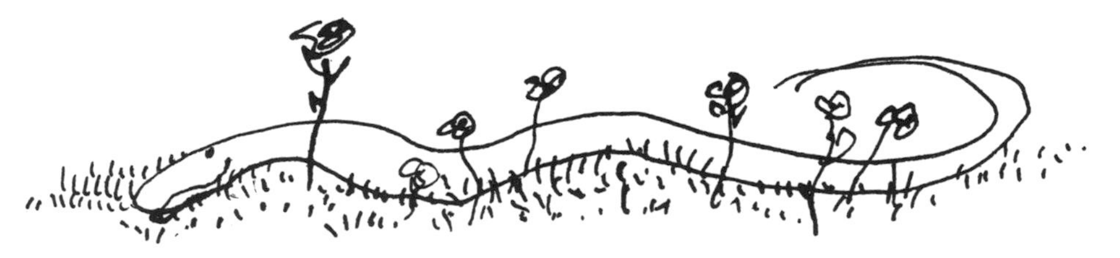

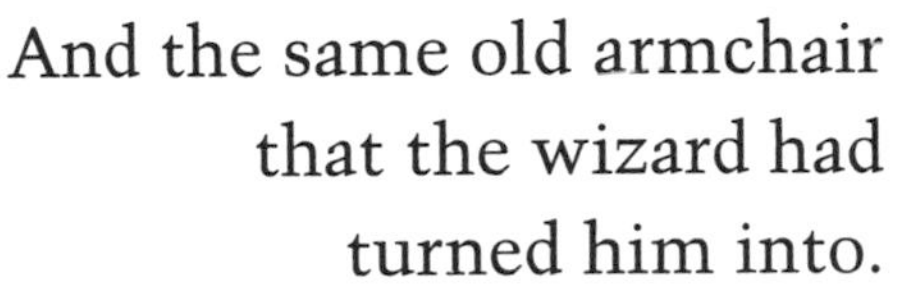
And the same old armchair
that the wizard had
turned him into.

The wanderers of the Forever Forest were never to know that the unamusing daisy, cow, snake, or armchair they passed within inches of was really Prince Roger.

At first, he spread his Magic Powder sparingly, wanting it to last. But soon he learned that, however much or little he threw on himself, the small pigskin sack was full again the next morning. Some spells lasted an hour, some a day, others a week or more. Roger didn't care; he enjoyed the change of pace.

"How come I never turn into a bird so I can fly out of this place?" he wondered to himself one day when he was a speckled trout playfully dodging the hooks of a couple of fishermen. He flapped his fins like a bird and went, "Cheep, cheep, cheep." The idea of being a fish who did bird imitations so charmed him that he swam to the surface to share his pleasure with the fishermen.

"Cheep, cheep, cheep," went Roger.

"Did you hear what I heard?" said the first fisherman, whose name was Colin the Carpenter.

"Tu-wit, tu-woo," went Roger, changing birdcalls.

"What do you think it is?" asked the second fisherman, whose name was Tim the Troubadour.

"It's either a bewitched bird or an unusually clever trout," said Colin the Carpenter.

"Cawww-cawww," went Roger.

"Can you do an owl?" shouted Tim the Troubadour.

"Woooo-woooo," went Roger.

"Don't go away!" cried the fishermen, and they ran off to fetch the rest of the forest dwellers.

So what started out to be one more boring day for the people of the Forever Forest turned into an unforgettable afternoon with a performing trout.

And so Roger made friends, and as the days turned into weeks, and the weeks into months, these new friends came to depend on him for the fun in their lives. When Roger appeared unexpectedly in one of his many guises—a talking frog, a dancing deer, a singing tree—they forgot about walking around in circles looking for a way home. If this had been a summer camp, he would have been the entertainment counselor.

One morning, Roger was wandering aimlessly about, charming the birds out of trees, when he heard, from afar, the deep-throated laughter of a man. Quickly, Roger splashed himself with Magic Powder and instantly turned into a boar. No sooner had he become this enormous, snorting, pawing, galumphing thing than he heard the swish of something ominous zipping past his right ear. An arrow embedded itself in the trunk of a tree less than an inch over his head. Roger the Boar whirled about to see charging toward him the hunter from the first chapter, who refused to leave this book when he should have, and got trapped in the Forever Forest instead.

"Stop or I'll shoot!" shouted the hunter. This was a stupid thing to say. Not only had he already shot, but he had an arrow fixed to his bow, ready to shoot again. Had Roger listened to him, he would have been a dead boar of a prince.

Fortunately, Roger knew exactly what to do. He lowered his head, snorted scarily, and charged the hunter as if he intended to kill him, which wasn't the case at all. He just wanted to play.

The chase went on for two hours, until both boar and hunter dropped from exhaustion.

"Don't kill me!" pleaded the hunter.

"Why should I kill you? I haven't had such a good time in ages," panted Roger.

The hunter was startled to hear a friendly voice coming out of such a beast. "Forgive me! I would not have taken a shot had I known you were enchanted. What are you, really? A prince?"

"It doesn't matter," said Roger, too modest to admit it.

"Whatever you are, you must be a noble creature to let me live. I'll never shoot a boar again, because it might be you. I'll only shoot stag."

Roger let out a hoot. "I might be a stag someday!"

"Then I will never again shoot boar *or* stag. I'll shoot . . . bear!"

"And what if *I* was that bear?" said Roger, pretending to sound indignant.

The hunter groaned. "Tell me what you won't be, so I can hunt *that*!"

"Anything!" Roger laughed uproariously. "I could be anything."

This news was taken gravely by the hunter. "I will never hunt again," said the man, who, though no longer a hunter, but still in this book, should have a name. How about Jack?

"I am Tom," said the former hunter, who will not do anything I tell him.

"I am Roger," said the boar.

"Tell me your story," said the former hunter. So they spent the next hour telling each other their stories, which you already know but can brush up on, if you like, by going back to Chapter 1.

Chapter 5

The Night of the Frogs

A note to the reader: This is my book. I am its author. I came up with a title I'm proud of because it sounds like poetry, which is good, and it isn't, which is better. I made up the story and all the characters—including Jack, who calls himself Tom—and that, I must admit, really frustrates me.

The neat thing about being a writer is that you know everything that's going to happen before it happens. In real life, you can't be sure of what's going to happen five minutes from now, but in your own book you're allowed to be in charge in a way that real life doesn't permit. And that's why people like me decide to be writers instead of, say, President. Because not even the President knows what a writer knows, which is what's going to happen next.

But this Jack who calls himself Tom comes along and, first, he won't get out of the book when he's supposed to and, next, he meets Roger and becomes his best friend. Yes, that's what happens next. I know, because I planned it that way. Not for this Jack to become Roger's best friend, but another hunter who I would have called Jack, and he would have *been* Jack if this fool hadn't come out of the woods first. Infuriating!

Anyhow, I just had to take this short break to complain. And don't worry, I'm still *mostly* in charge of this story, and it should go pretty much as I plan. But be careful about this Tom. Yes, I'm going to call him Tom. I have no choice because that's what Roger calls him, and it would be confusing if I called him one name and Roger called him another.

One final word: Don't trust Tom. And if you run into him anywhere outside this book, don't tell him I told you so.

Thank you.

Go on to the next chapter, which will also be 5. This wasn't really Chapter 5, and there is no "Night of the Frogs." I just called it that to fool Tom.

Chapter 5
Tom

How did Roger and Tom come to be best friends? They weren't at all alike. Tom was a peasant, Roger was a prince. Tom was five years older, a fully grown man. Roger was a young man, in most ways still a boy. Tom had a wife and son, although he had not seen them since he got stuck in the Forever Forest. He had pretty much forgotten them, and they him. A year after his disappearance, his wife petitioned King Whatchamacallit for a royal decree declaring her husband dead. Within a month, she was married to the next-door farmer, a kind, decent, reliable fellow named Jack, of all things, who I'd rather be writing about than Tom. But Jack can't be in this book because he never got to know Roger. While Tom was his best friend. Life is tricky that way. Not everything is how you'd want it.

Roger had grown up without anyone to play with. His friends back at the palace laughed too hard to be able to play with him. And his friends in the Forever Forest were too old to do anything but be entertained. Tom was a different story. Tom was close enough to Roger's age to have fun with, especially after a splash of J. Wellington Wizard's Magic Powder. For fun and games, Roger turned himself into everything and anything: plants, animals, furniture, puddles.

By itself, there's nothing funny about a puddle, but with Tom jumping up and down in it and Roger splashing mud all over Tom . . . that sort of good time draws two people together.

Another favorite was a hiding game called hot-and-cold, which they played only when Roger turned into something, like a stick or a rock, that Tom could pick up and throw. The way this game worked was that Tom had to hurl Roger with all his might into the thickest part of the woods, and then go look for him.

"Am I hot or cold?" cried Tom, trekking through the woods, trek, trek, trek.

"Ice-cold," said Roger in little more than a whisper, so as not to give his location away.

Tom changed directions. "Am I getting warmer?"

"You're freezing! You've got frostbite! You're an icicle!" cried Roger, who happened, on this occasion, to be a horseshoe buried in a mound of pine needles.

And so the afternoon wore on, with Tom stumbling here and there and back, hunting down his buddy. "Am I warmer?"

"Hot!"

"Am I still hot?"

"You're burning up!"

"I've got you!"

It was hard for Roger to imagine a better time. How could Tom not be his best friend?

After a long day's fun and games, Roger and Tom liked to relax and talk things over, which is what friends usually do, but never Roger. To him, this was a totally new experience. "We should come up with a plan," Roger said one day when he was a tree. He looked forward to these late-afternoon chats.

"Why do we need a plan?" asked Tom, who sat in Roger's shade, fishing a brook for their supper.

"A plan to get us out of here," said Roger.

"This is the Forever Forest. We are here forever," said Tom.

Roger knew that couldn't be true because he was on a quest. "I don't believe that," he said.

"I'm older than you, so I know better."

"But I'm a prince, so it's only right that I should know better."

"A peasant who has seen life knows better than a

prince who's been cooped up in a tower so he won't make people laugh," said Tom.

"A prince is educated and a peasant is not. You can't read," said Roger.

"What good is it to read in a forest without books?" asked Tom.

Tom had a point, but Roger didn't want to give in. "You're just jealous because I'm educated."

"If you're so educated, what kind of tree are you?" sneered Tom. Roger was stumped. "I know what kind of tree you are, and you do-hon't," Tom chanted in a singsong voice.

"I'm not a real tree, anyhow, so why should I care?"

"Good, because I'm not telling you-hoo," chanted Tom.

"Good, because I know something about you that I'm not tell-helling," chanted back Roger.

"No, you do-hon't," chanted Tom.

"Yes, I do-hoo," chanted Roger.

"You're making it uh-hup because you want me to tell you what kind of tree-hee you are-har," chanted Tom.

"No, I'm nah-hot," sang Roger.

Tom had run out of patience. "You tell me, then I'll tell you."

"First, you have to tell me."

"First, you tell me."

"First, you tell me!" No one could outlast Roger at being silly.

"You're a maple," Tom growled. "Now it's your turn."

"One of my branches is about to fall on your head."

One second earlier, and Tom might have had time to duck. "Ouch!" he cried, as a low-hanging branch fell off Roger, who laughed so hard that his leaves fluttered as if in applause.

"That's not funny," whined Tom, rubbing his sore head.

"It's funny to *me*!"

"How would you like it if I kicked you?" said Tom, too irritated to remember that he was threatening a tree, not a prince.

"I don't care,
You should care,
You wear your mother's underwear,"
replied Roger in singsong.

So Tom kicked Roger and sprained his toe. He limped off into the forest with the fish he had caught. "Catch your own dinner!" he shouted.

Roger could barely stop laughing long enough to shout back: "Trees don't eat fish! If you were educated, you'd know that!"

But an hour later he had stopped being a tree and was hungry for fish. Tom was off somewhere sulking and eating, while Roger had to content himself with apples and berries for dinner. That taught him a lesson. "I'll have to be more careful about what I laugh at. What a shame," he lamented.

Chapter 6

The Best Party on the Face of the Earth

Saturday was party night in the Forever Forest. Large Lucille was in charge of the feast. Thirty years ago, on the day before her wedding, Little Lucille (as she was then) played hide-and-seek with her sweetheart, Andrew.

"Ready or not, here I come!" Andrew shouted after counting to a hundred. But he didn't find her. Little Lucille had hidden behind a tree in the Forever Forest. Once in, never out. Lucille didn't know that. Another thing she didn't know was that Andrew went off to seek her in the wrong direction—and was still seeking her thirty years later. "Come out, come out, wherever you are!" he had been heard to shout in 23,568 villages on five continents.

Of course, Lucille hadn't the foggiest notion of any of this. All she knew on that fateful day thirty years ago was that, after hiding for ten hours behind a tree, she was cold and cramped and annoyed with Andrew for not finding her.

So she came out from behind the tree, only to realize that she was in a forest from which there was no escape. "But I'm getting married tomorrow," she moaned. But she wasn't. Not that tomorrow, or 11,000 tomorrows thereafter.

So she ate. And she ate and she ate.

And she ate and she ate and she ate.

Perhaps with the idea that if she couldn't find her way out, she could eat her way out. But that didn't happen, either. All that happened was that Little Lucille blossomed into Large Lucille, adored by the wandering citizens of the Forever Forest for her lavish Saturday-night feasts. They would eat until they could eat no more, then Lucille would eat their leftovers.

Once Roger had come to live in the forest, Lucille's Saturday-night feasts changed significantly. After everybody stuffed themselves with roast duck, roast pheasant, roast turkey, roast pig, roast venison, roast beef, roast bear, and the fixings, after they chatted and sang all the old songs and reminisced about their former lives, Fred the Farmer, Polly the Peasant, Peter the Peasant, Sarah the Seamstress, Belle the Barmaid, Colin the Carpenter, Ingrid the Innkeeper, Paul the Porter, Patrick the Papermaker, Michael the Merchant, Tim the Troubadour, Millicent the Match Girl, and dozens of others settled down with an air of anticipation. They waited.

What were they waiting for? At around eleven o'clock, Tom stepped out of the darkness into their circle. "Is everybody here?" he shouted.

"Yes!" shouted back the citizens of the Forever Forest.

Tom cupped a hand to his ear and leaned forward into the circle. "I can't hear youuuu!" he shouted.

"YESSSS!" The word filled the Forever Forest like a thousand balloons losing air.

"Are we ready for Prince Roger?" Tom cried, raising his voice a notch higher.

"YESSSSS!" came back the passionate hiss of the lost wanderers.

Tom took a step back from the crowd and nodded and winked to old friends. "Do we have any new faces here tonight?" He picked out an unfamiliar face in the crowd. "Sir, I haven't seen you before."

"I got lost a week ago," said a young, redheaded man,

the fuzz of a new beard growing on his chin.

"A week ago! How about that?" Tom grinned mischievously at his fellow Forever Forest veterans who'd been lost for so many years that a week seemed like a minute to them. They laughed, hooted, and applauded the stranger. Tom quieted the crowd with a wave of his hand.

"May I ask where you are from, sir?"

"The kingdom of good King Whatchamacallit!"

"How about that, that's Prince Roger's father!" Tom looped his right fist in circles over his head.

"Ro*ger*! Ro*ger*! Ro*ger*!" As the Forever Forest people sang out his name, they began to snicker, chuckle, giggle, then laugh. Prince Roger was approaching. A half mile away . . . a quarter mile . . . an eighth of a mile . . . and then he was in their midst! Sheep sleeping in meadows miles away raised their heads in wonder at the distant sound of cheers and laughter. Latecomers ran, stumbled, and scrambled from all directions to reach what was obviously the best party on the face of the earth.

Fifteen minutes later, as it became clear to Roger that the partygoers were near total collapse, he did what he did

at every party: he splashed himself with Magic Powder and vanished. And no one but Tom suspected that he was that spider or that squirrel or that tree stump or that toadstool, or whichever of the hundreds of animals, vegetables, and furniture he turned himself into during his years of contentment in the Forever Forest. His quest was long forgotten. His single care now was to make the people of the Forever Forest, once a week for fifteen minutes, feel lucky to be lost.

Chapter 7
Abraca . . .

Meanwhile, back at the castle, J. Wellington Wizard seethed with frustration, ferment, and fury. He fussed, he fretted, he fidgeted, he slept fitfully. Three years had passed since he sent Roger out on his quest. Three years! And where was he and what was he doing? He was in the Forever Forest, being the life of the party!

Once a week the wizard checked his crystal ball to see if there was any change; that is, once a week for the first year, once a month for the second year, twice a year for the third year. And what did he see in his crystal ball? Roger up to his old tricks: causing people to laugh so hard and so often that they forgot the sorry state of their existence. They forgot that they were lost, wandering around in circles, getting nowhere. They were happy, of all things! And Roger was happy! Only J. Wellington Wizard was miserable.

At the end of the first year, King Whatchamacallit summoned his most wise and trusted counselor to the Royal Quarters. "What do you son of my hear on the quest? I mean, what do you quest of my hear on the son? I mean, what do you hear of my son on the quest?"

J. Wellington could not break his kind king's heart by telling him the truth. "I have nothing to report," he reported.

"Nothing?"

"Nothing."

At the end of the second year, King Whatchamacallit summoned his most faithful and brilliant counselor to the Royal Quarters. "What do you hear of my quest on the son? No, what do you quest of my son on the moon? That's not it. What do you son of my son on the son? That's wrong—"

For so long a question, J. Wellington Wizard had a short, unhappy answer: "Nothing."

"Whating?"

"Nothing, Your Highness."

"Nothing? Can ears believe my I?"

By the end of the third year, King Whatchamacallit had lost faith in his old friend.

J. Wellington slunk off from his interview. What was there for the poor man to say? He had checked his crystal ball that morning. Roger had turned himself into a bear and chased Tom up a tree. Tom broke off branches of the tree and threw them at Roger, who caught them in his teeth, gnawed off the bark, and roared, "More!" Not at all the behavior of a prince on a quest, thought the great wizard.

He had sent Roger into the Forever Forest in the hope that he would take his first steps toward becoming a man and figure his way out. Some joke. But J. Wellington couldn't laugh, it hurt too much. Particularly when he thought of the tradition of the quest, the *grandeur* of the quest: tens of thousands of quests down through history proving the courage, the heroism of kings, princes, knights, and mere lads. Fighting dragons, hydra-headed monsters, sea serpents, ogres, witches, wizards . . .

Well, here was a wizard . . . J. Wellington Wizard! Helpless, humiliated. By the beloved son of his beloved king, no less! J. Wellington scowled, he simmered, he sulked, he growled. He kicked the cat. The cat clawed him. The scratch became infected. J. Wellington took to his bed. His fever rose. His powers shrunk. His will to live shrunk. He hovered between life and death, vainly trying, in his delirium, to remember the incantation for infected scratches. He was able to remember "Abraca—" but nothing further. "Abracawhat? Abracawhich? Abracawhazzis? Abracawhatchamacallit?"

Thinking like the king made him think he was the king, which made him weep for his lost son, Roger. For seven days and nights his fever rose and fell and rose again. He wept, he slept, he woke, he said, "Abra—abraca—abracasomething—" But the last part of the incantation would not come. Or, when it did, it arrived just before sleep, before he could pronounce the final syllable that would bring him back to health: "Abracadab—"

He slept a long, tortured, raging sleep. And woke weak and weary, without the dimmest recollection of

how to end the incantation. "Abracathis—abracathat—abracaup—abracadown—abracaout—abracain—abraca-IwishIweredead." And he almost was. He came this close.

One day King Whatchamacallit came to visit. "I sick you've been hear!" he said, terribly upset. "I've son my lost, don't lose me let you!" he cried, too distraught to untie his sentences. "Magic isn't there you use can? Cure? Something say? Dabraca abra? *You* know!"

And J. Wellington knew! The king, in his foolish, senseless way, had reminded him. True, he said it backwards, but what so?

"Abracadabra!" J. Wellington Wizard gasped with the last of his voice, the last of his wit, the last of his failing strength. And then, seconds later, he was his old self. And was he sore at Roger!

Chapter 8

The Wizard's Revenge

Roger woke to the distant sound of Tom's giggling. Tom lived a little over a mile away in a little thatched hut in the woods, exactly like the one Roger lived in. Tom had built Roger's hut and then had built one for himself almost a mile "outside the perimeter of laughter," as Tom liked to call it. Each morning on rising, Tom stuffed a sack with eggs, fruit, and berries for Roger and himself and then started trekking through the woods—trek, trek, trek—to the young prince's hut.

Being of noble birth, Roger slept later than Tom, and might have slept through the day had he not been awakened by the approaching giggle. Tom's giggle was Roger's wake-up call. Before it swelled into an uncontrollable roar, Roger was off his bed of straw, splashed three or four parts of his body with water from the cold spring, and climbed into the same tattered garments he had worn since his arrival in the Forever Forest.

It was Roger's routine, after rising, to take out his sack of Magic Powder, sprinkle himself, and turn into some-

thing safe and somber that neither Tom nor anyone else could get a laugh out of. But this morning was different. This morning, Roger was shocked to discover that his sack of Magic Powder was half empty.

Something was wrong. No matter how much Magic Powder Roger had used the day before, he always found his sack full the next morning. Because it was magic, and *he* was a prince, Roger took it for granted that he would never use his powder up.

Tom was coming closer, laughing harder. Roger should definitely have turned into a cow or a snake by now. But he didn't. He couldn't. He was too stunned by the diminished bag of Magic Powder to move. "What does this mean?" he thought. His first thought in a long time. The last time he came close to thinking was when he was a tree and dropped a branch on Tom's head. In the course of a day, thinking was at the bottom of his list of things to do. Why think when you can play?

"Ha-ha-ha-ha-ha." Tom's loud laugh was nearly upon

him. Roger did nothing. He stood frozen, staring foolishly into the half-empty bag of Magic Powder, saying over and over to himself, "What does this mean?"

I'm not allowed to tell Roger what it means because that would interfere with our story, but there's no reason why I can't tell you. J. Wellington Wizard was taking his revenge. He was not going to go through all that illness and humiliation without punishing Roger. So he decided that the worst thing he could do, which was also the best thing he could do, was to take away his bag of Magic Powder. In that way, Roger would be punished as he deserved—and he would be forced, like it or not, to stop dawdling and get on with his quest. This explains the fix Roger now found himself in.

"Ha-ha-ha!" roared Tom. "I'm about to *ha-ha-ha* die *ha-ha-ha* laughing *ha-ha-ha*. You'd better do *ha-ha-ha* something *ha-ha-ha*."

Only then did Roger remember what he was supposed to do at a time like this. With great care, he sprinkled on himself ten flakes of leftover Magic Powder. Instantly, he was turned into a toad. Instantly, Tom stopped laughing.

"What am I?" Roger asked Tom. Since he was inside whatever thing or creature he had turned into, he had no way of knowing what it was.

"A toad," said Tom.

"Darn! Darn! Darn!" said Roger. "I was hoping I'd turn into something wise that could think. Like a wise old owl."

"Why would you want to think on such a beautiful day?"

So Roger told him about the Magic Powder. "What am I going to do?" Roger asked his friend.

"*What* are you going to do? What *are* you going to do? What are *you* going to do? What are you *going* to do? What are you going to *do*?" Having run out of ways to repeat himself, Tom looked up at the sky as if it might tell him what Roger was going to do.

Ten minutes later, he looked down. "*I* know," he said with a surly grin. When Tom had the edge on Roger, he enjoyed rubbing it in.

"What? *What?*" demanded Roger.

Tom furrowed his brow, pursed his lips, and pressed an index finger up against his chin. "You have to make a decision."

"A decision?" groaned Roger. "But I've never made a decision."

"There's always a first time."

"I've never *had* to make a decision before."

"Think of it as a challenge," said Tom, from between pursed lips.

"How do you go about it?" asked Roger.

Tom started to say something and stopped. Then he started to say something else and stopped again. Then, not knowing what he was going to say, he said it anyway. "You just— You put together all the— You think this way and that— You make a list— You weigh the alternatives—" Tom fell silent. "I'm a peasant," he said at last. "I've never had to make a decision. People like you are supposed to make them for me."

"What if I make one—and it's wrong?"

"I'm not an expert, but if a decision doesn't work out, my guess would be that you have to make another decision."

"A *second* decision?" cried Roger in alarm.

"I'm not an expert, but my guess would be you keep

making decisions until you get one that works."

"That could take *years*!" said Roger the Toad.

"That's another reason why I don't make them."

"But if I don't make one, what will happen?"

Tom giggled. "You'll run out of Magic Powder."

"*Then* what?"

"Everyone will laugh himself to death, including me." Tom started to laugh in anticipation.

"So then I don't have a choice, do I?"

Tom stopped laughing. "Sorry, but I'm in over my head. This is more thinking than I'm used to."

"I'm exhausted," said Roger.

Tom nodded. "You and me both."

The two friends, man and toad, closed their eyes. Roger was trying to think. During the wait, Tom practiced furrowing his brow and pursing his lips.

Chapter 9
Farewell to the Forever Forest

After a week of thinking and getting nowhere, Roger decided that he had to get somewhere. And that somewhere was out of the Forever Forest. Because if he didn't, his dear friends, including his closest friend in the world, Tom, would die laughing the moment he ran out of Magic Powder. And that moment was but a day or two away. So Roger made up a message that he urged Tom to memorize so that he could tell it to their friends.

"I have a decision to make," Tom recited to the assembled forest dwellers, repeating the words exactly as Roger had composed them. "I have to be alone to make my decision. I cannot see you again until I have made my decision. Please go deep into the Forever Forest, at least a mile. Don't come back until Tom says it's all right. I will tell Tom when it's all right, and he will tell you. He'll know right after I know, and then you'll know. I apologize for the inconvenience. Please don't be mad at me, as if you could. Signed: Your friend, Roger."

Roger was more alone now than he ever remembered

being, even back in the tower. He sat on the bank of a brook staring at his toes in the water. He tried, really tried, for a decision, but all he could manage to come up with was how funny his toes looked underwater, like ten little worms standing on line.

He thought for hours about his toes, how foolish toes looked, his little toe more foolish than the rest, as if it were attached to his foot as an afterthought. If his little toe were on the opposite side of his foot, would it look less foolish? He wondered about that. If the toes on his feet were in the opposite order, would he walk in reverse? He wondered about that. And then he wondered, if he were to walk in reverse, was it possible that he would walk out of the Forever Forest?

"When I walk forward," he thought, "the Forever Forest gets deeper and deeper, so if I walk backward, why shouldn't it be the opposite? And if not, why not?" And not knowing how he had come to it—and certainly not having planned it—Roger found that he had made a decision. His very first.

He took his feet out of the water and shook them dry. Then he put on his boots and took a step backward. Then a second step. Then a third. He was tempted to look behind to see where he was going, but he made a second decision, which was: *Don't*. For the rest of that day, he walked backward. And all of the next and all of the next and all of the next day. And at the end of the fifth day he noticed, as he backed up, that his feet were no longer on grass, they were on rock. "Rock?" he thought. But he didn't look back. He looked in front of him. The trail he had just passed through was bathed in sunlight. Unblocked sunlight, the likes of which Roger had not seen in years. No trees throwing shadows, no shrubs or brambles or flowers, no overarching canopy of thick, damp-smelling pine.

No greens! No greens anywhere! "Should I look behind me?" he thought. Better not. Instead, he backed up. The sun beat mercilessly down on him, and this he was not used to. He had been in the shade for three years.

He tried to take in his new surroundings, which is hard to do when you are walking backward, because if you don't concentrate on what you're doing you lose your balance and fall down. Try it, if you don't believe me.

Roger tried it, and he found it hard. He nearly fell down a couple of times, so what he did was stop for a moment and take a peek. A little peek to the side, plus a tiny squint behind. Another peek, another squint, another step. And so on. Until he had a pretty good idea of where he was. Nowhere.

He had backed into the middle of nowhere. Nothing to see anywhere but rock. Flat gray rock. Flat brown rock. As he backed up, he thought, "What a joke! I've gone from the Forever Forest to the Forever Rock. I wonder if I'll ever see my friends again."

If there was anyone to see he would have seen him, because wherever he looked, it was flat, it was open, it was rock. Nothing was there to be seen. Not a person, not a castle, not a hut, not a tree, not a bush, not a bird. Only rocks, and more rocks. Flat as the eye could see. Apparently in every direction, although Roger couldn't be sure because he would have to turn around to be sure. And he was afraid to do that. He was afraid that if he turned and looked, he would find the Forever Forest.

This didn't make sense, but he believed it anyway. Whatever his eyes told him, he believed that behind him there remained a forest. And he could stay out of it only if he walked backward. And this he did, for the rest of that day and far into the night, although he was weak and hungry and would have liked nothing better than to lie down and go to sleep on the last slab of rock he had backed over.

But he didn't. He couldn't. The night grew dark. The air turned chilly. Not only was Roger tired and weak and hungry, he was freezing cold. His teeth chattered. This amused him, his teeth had never chattered before. Listening to the rhythm of his teeth caused him to forget how cold he was: fast, then slow, then change of beat. Roger's entire body, especially his teeth, began to feel like a musical instrument. Tik-atiktik tik atikety-tik-tik. Faster. Slower. Mix it up. Tiktik tickety-tik. What fun! Roger was just beginning to get into a fast-tempo composition for the teeth—the sound was truly exciting!—when he backed off the edge of a cliff.

He laughed for an hour. And why not? He was alive! Dangling helplessly from a narrow spit of rock one hundred feet below the cliff he had just walked off. Fortunately for Roger, his plunge had been halted by his tunic billowing out and catching onto this lifesaving rock.

Otherwise: straight to the bottom—*splat!*—like Wile E. Coyote. Except he wouldn't have been alive in the next scene, because this is a book, not an animated cartoon, so I have to be more realistic.

To and fro he swung in
space, in a rhythm that
was syncopated with the
clicking of his teeth.
To and fro, back and forth,
body swinging, teeth clicking.
In the blackness of the night,
knowing nothing of where he
was—how high, how low?—
Roger felt strangely
secure, like an infant in
a cradle. True, he was
exhausted; true, his
life hung by a thread.
Nonetheless,
he fell asleep
with a smile
on his face.

Chapter 10
Lady Sadie

"You down there! Yes, I'm talking to you!"

This is precisely how Roger was awakened. By a plain-looking, plainspoken woman named Lady Sadie, who

stood on the edge of the cliff observing the beautiful sunrise (which Roger missed entirely because he was fast asleep).

Lady Sadie was in service to the allegedly beautiful Princess Petulia. *Alleged* is a legal term. Lawyers use it: the alleged bank robber, the alleged diamond smuggler, the alleged mugger. It means that this is what certain people think is true, although no one has proved it yet. No one could prove that Princess Petulia was beautiful because no one had seen her up close since she was a baby. She wore a veil. Take off the veil, it was said, and one would find a beauty so astonishing that it actually turned men to stone. But no one had ever seen Petulia behind her veil. So, while everyone in her kingdom and beyond spoke of her paralyzing beauty, there wasn't any proof.

Why am I telling you this now, when Roger is dangling in midair and, anyhow, it's way ahead of my story? I guess I was trying to explain why Petulia was an *alleged* beauty. And I hope I have. Now, where was I? Oh yes, Roger was waking up to this strange woman yelling down at him as he's hanging by the skirt of his tunic from a cliff.

It took Roger only a moment to recognize his peril. It had been dark when he walked backward off the cliff, so he couldn't see how far he had fallen or how much further he might yet fall. And he was too tired to worry about it. But now, after a good night's sleep, he was rested enough to understand his plight.

Take a look and you too will understand his plight.

The plain-looking, plainspoken Lady Sadie didn't give a fig for Roger's plight. She had her own problems. Right now, her problem was that an astonishingly beautiful necklace given her by her (allegedly) astonishingly beautiful princess had slipped off while she was standing by the edge of the cliff admiring the sunrise. It had dropped over the cliff onto Roger's neck. Where it now hung as he swung. To and fro. Back and forth. "If you hand me my necklace, I will be on my way!" shouted Lady Sadie.

"I would if I could, but I can't!" Roger shouted back. "Because I've fallen off a cliff and I can't get up."

"A likely story," sniffed Lady Sadie.

"True, but I'm not responsible for it," said Roger.

He was right, of course. *I* am responsible for it. And having got him into this mess, I've introduced Lady Sadie to help him out. Not that she was interested in saving Roger. But she did want to retrieve her necklace.

Years ago, before she became a lady, Lady Sadie had worked as a tightrope walker in the circus. Though she had achieved a far higher station in life—lady-in-waiting to an astonishingly beautiful princess—still, she went nowhere without her tightrope. It took no more than a quick twist of her wrists to expertly knot one end of her tightrope to a stone at the top of the cliff and drop the rest of the line down to Roger. "Tie my necklace to the rope, and I'll pull it up!" she shouted.

"I'll tie myself to the rope, and you can pull us both up!" Roger called to her.

"Can't you do as I ask?" complained Lady Sadie.

"Why should I give you your necklace if you don't

pull me up?" shouted Roger.

"Why shouldn't you give me my necklace when it doesn't belong to you?" shouted back Lady Sadie.

"*You* dropped it!" responded Roger.

"What pleasure does it give you to wear my necklace, hanging from the ledge of a cliff?" reasoned Lady Sadie. "Why does everything with men have to be so complicated?"

"I don't believe you want your necklace as much as you say," argued Roger. "Otherwise, you'd pull me up."

"I do want it! It's mine!" Tears of frustration welled in Lady Sadie's eyes.

"But I'm wearing it, so it's mine." Roger had never looked so determined.

"But it will be mine again if you tie it to the end of the rope!" cried Lady Sadie.

"It will only be yours again if I tie me *and* the necklace to the end of the rope!" cried back Roger.

"You and the necklace are too heavy. First, send up the necklace, *then* I'll make an effort to pull you up."

What Roger didn't realize was that for the first time in his life he was bargaining. Being of royal blood, he didn't have to bargain, he just got what he wanted. But now he was learning fast: If you have something somebody wants, like a necklace, and they have something you want, like a rope, you bargain back and forth until you reach an agreement.

Lady Sadie was a tough bargainer, but Roger had the upper hand. Although she was in danger of losing her necklace, he was in danger of plummeting headfirst to the canyon floor. So he was bargaining for his life. Still and all, it took till the middle of the afternoon for her to give in. And not at all gracefully.

As she hauled on the rope and Roger clambered up the face of the cliff, she muttered under her breath: "The most unreasonable, most irritating, most nasty person I have ever had the bad fortune to meet. Once he's up, I will seize my necklace and push him back over." Now, she didn't mean that, she was just mad that she lost the argument. And she stayed mad until the very last tug on the rope, when she and Roger came face to face. At which point, Lady Sadie burst out laughing and didn't stop until Roger remembered his Magic Powder and sprinkled a tiny portion of what remained on himself.

Once she stopped laughing, Lady Sadie took a look around, but she saw no Roger. "Too ashamed to show your face in public!" she cried to the skies. Then she grabbed her necklace off the neck of the adorable Labrador puppy that sat wagging its tail at her, and stalked off among the rocks.

Chapter 11
The Dastardly Divide

Rocks. Big rocks. Little rocks. Medium-sized rocks. Nothing but rocks as far as the eye could see, which, if you looked in one direction, was to the cliff Roger had walked off. A distance away, almost a half mile across the canyon floor, stood another mountain. More rocks, big, little, medium. And after that a precipice, another canyon, another mountain, and yet more rocks. Small wonder this was known as the Dastardly Divide. Once on, never off. Unless you happened to be a bird. But no birds came to the Dastardly Divide. Because birds cannot feed off rocks. And that was all there was on the Dastardly Divide. No trees, no fields, no streams, no vegetation. Just rocks.

People can't feed off rocks any better than birds. Roger was hungry. Ten days on the Dastardly Divide, and he had lost weight, he had lost color, he had turned gray. He looked like a tall, skinny rock. This didn't affect his good humor, but it diminished its range. Thus, he was able to approach within one hundred feet of Lady Sadie without making her laugh. Or even smile. Another few feet, and she would have fallen under his spell, or what remained of it in his starved condition. But now she reclined in the shadow of a large rock, chewing on a little rock for nourishment. She didn't have a clue that Roger was there, or she wouldn't have spoken as she did—that is, to the rock she was gnawing on. "You aren't nearly as tasty as the rock I chewed yesterday. That was the best rock ever! It was cool as the morning dew. Not that you are the worst rock I've gnawed on, but I am a plain-spoken woman, and I must say that you will never fool anyone into thinking that you are a rock of the first order."

"Lady Sadie!" called Roger from exactly one hundred feet away. "We have to get away from here or we'll die!"

"I don't like to talk while I'm eating!" snapped Lady Sadie. But she wasn't really eating and it took only a moment for her to realize that. "So there you are! Why are you standing so far away? Where have you been hiding? Are you afraid that I'll eat you?" She threw away the rock she was nibbling on. At Roger, actually, but she missed.

"I wasn't hiding. I was the Labrador puppy—and if I come any closer, you'll laugh," said Roger.

"Don't make me laugh!" snorted Lady Sadie.

"I won't," said Roger, "unless I come closer, which isn't a good idea because if you're laughing how can we talk about how I have to get out of here?"

"You're not the only one who has to get out of here," said Lady Sadie.

"Sure, but you have to get out of here only because you want to survive, I have to get out of here because I'm on a quest."

"I have to get out of here because I must find a knight or a prince or somebody like that to rescue my princess, Princess Petulia, who's astonishingly beautiful and who's been kidnapped by a giant."

"That sounds like it could be a quest!" said Roger, astonished that another quest was in the works at the same time as his own.

"Are you a knight?" challenged Lady Sadie. She knew that he wasn't.

"No," said Roger.

"Are you a prince?" challenged Lady Sadie. She knew that he wasn't.

"Yes, I am a prince."

"You're no prince."

"I am so a prince," insisted Roger.

"You mean when you're a Labrador puppy? Here, Prince. Good, Prince. Sit, Prince. Roll over. That kind of prince? No, thank you," growled Lady Sadie.

"I was born a prince and I'll die a prince. I've just had a string of bad luck lately. My name is Roger."

"The prince who makes everyone laugh?"

"That's me."

"You don't make me laugh. I think you're lying."

"If I came closer, you'd laugh."

"No, I wouldn't."

"Yes, you would." And Roger stepped closer and Lady Sadie laughed. "You laughed," said Roger.

"I laughed at the ridiculous idea that you could be a prince. That's why I laughed. And don't you think it's for any other reason."

Roger sighed. "I never knew anyone who argued so much."

"I don't argue," argued Lady Sadie. "I'm just plainspoken. I was born plain and was raised plainspoken. If I was born pretty, like Princess Petulia, I could make my way in the world without being plainspoken. But I wasn't, so I can't and I don't."

Roger studied Lady Sadie. "Actually, you're kind of—well—pretty."

"I'm plain-looking, and don't you dare tell me otherwise!" Lady Sadie glared at Roger in her plain way, but for once did not argue. Roger was grateful for the silence. When she spoke again, her tone was different and so was her demeanor. Both were softer. "I can be pretty in a certain light. Let me see." She checked out the sky and the placement of the sun and the length of the shadows that fell off the jagged rocks. "Yes, this is sort of the hour for kind of the light for me to look more or less pretty in. Pretty for me, that is. Almost. Not quite. Close. There—the light's gone. Just as well, now I look like myself again. Plain."

Roger didn't see any difference between the light now and the light of a minute ago. To him, Lady Sadie looked the same.

"I think you look perfectly all right," said Roger.

"I don't like to discuss my looks. You think I look perfectly all right?"

"Absolutely."

"Not plain?"

"That's not the way I'd put it."

"'Perfectly all right' would be the way you'd put it?"

"'Perfectly all right' is right," said Roger.

Lady Sadie frowned. "I'm not sure it's not better to be truly plain-looking than merely perfectly all right." All the softness that Roger had noticed a bit earlier was gone. Like magic. Like him turning into a Labrador puppy.

Roger sighed. "We'd better talk about getting out of here."

Chapter 12
Farewell to the Dastardly Divide

How long can you suck on rocks without becoming disheartened? Not long. Two weeks on the Dastardly Divide left Roger and Lady Sadie so thin that their clothes hung off them.

And far less talkative. They didn't have to talk much. What was there left to say? They were on their way to dying. But not fast. Not so fast that they couldn't make plans on how not to die.

"You're a tightrope walker, right?" Roger said one morning as he sorted out rocks, looking for a good one.

"I was," said Lady Sadie. "But that was before I became lady-in-waiting." She picked up a rock Roger had tossed aside. "You're so fussy," she said and began chewing on it.

"What if we threw your rope across the Dastardly Divide to the other side and you walked across it and then you pulled me over? How's that for a plan?"

"Terrible," snapped Lady Sadie. "How come it's always up to me to rescue you and not the other way around?"

Roger grinned. Lady Sadie's plainspokenness never failed to amuse him.

"I couldn't throw a rope a half mile, and neither could you," growled Lady Sadie. "And if I could or you could, tell me who's on the other side to tie it taut so that I could walk across? If I had the strength, which I don't."

"You're right." Roger sighed. "Okay, it's your turn."

"My turn for what?"

"To come up with a plan. Why do I have to come up with all the plans?"

"I don't have a plan because I don't have an imagination. I'm far too plainspoken and plain-thinking, and just as well, I say, because *your* plans get us nowhere."

"You wouldn't think they were so terrible if I thought of one that worked."

"If you did, I'd be pleasantly surprised. And I am never pleasantly surprised. Whenever I'm surprised I'm *unpleas-*

antly surprised. Like when the giant ran off with Princess Petulia, that was an unpleasant surprise. And when I sought to find a knight or a prince to rescue her and found myself trapped in the Dastardly Divide, that was an unpleasant surprise. And then I met you."

"Am I an unpleasant surprise?" asked Roger, hoping that he wasn't.

"I may be plainspoken, but not so plainspoken that I'd insult you to your face."

"Thank you," said Roger, taking that as a compliment.

Lady Sadie silently sucked on her rock. She didn't know what to make of Roger's "Thank you." No one had thanked her in her entire life. In all her years, she had not once been called upon to say "You're welcome." Until she met Roger. "You're welcome," she grunted.

But Roger didn't hear. His mind was elsewhere. "Say, could saving Princess Petulia from the giant be my quest?"

The plainspoken Lady Sadie was about to say "Are you out of your mind?" when she remembered Roger's "Thank you" and restrained herself.

"Maybe you and I met so I could hear about Princess Petulia, who I will rescue from the giant and she'll lift her veil and I'll make her laugh and I won't turn to stone and we'll get married. What do you think?"

"You're welcome," said Lady Sadie for the second time in her life, unable to think of anything else to say that wasn't an insult.

"I have a plan!" cried Roger.

"No!" moaned Lady Sadie in despair.

It was Roger's last plan but should have been his first. It was so simple he couldn't imagine why he hadn't come up with it before. His Magic Powder!

His bag was nearly empty, but there were about two pinches left. Just enough to sprinkle himself and—if there was any to spare—Lady Sadie. But there was a problem: If he sprinkled himself first, then whatever he turned into, he would be in no position to sprinkle Lady Sadie. So he had better sprinkle her first, he thought, and try to keep a little left over for himself.

This plan made good sense to Roger. It didn't occur to him that he had put Lady Sadie's interests before his own. This was a first! Quite a day for firsts: Roger's first consideration for anyone besides himself, Lady Sadie's first "You're welcome."

Now, when you're considerate of other people, it introduces a whole new set of problems. Thinking it over, Roger realized that if he were to explain to Lady Sadie that he wanted to sprinkle her with Magic Powder to change her into something or someone who might have a chance of escaping the Dastardly Divide, then one, and only one, consequence would follow: a long and futile argument. An argument that would amuse Roger, infuriate Lady Sadie, and end nowhere. Roger did not have the strength to go on ending nowhere, so he did what a lot of well-meaning peo-

ple do, including parents: He made the decision for Lady Sadie. Without consulting her. Behind her back, while she sucked noisily on a totally dry rock, making loud, unpleasant thwacking sounds, Roger took all but a few flakes of the last of the Magic Powder, ran the hundred feet to where she was huddled, and released the flakes over her frail and pitiful body.

Out of nowhere, a strong wind gusted from the east. "A lucky omen," thought Roger, because what Lady Sadie had turned into was a leaf.

"What have you done to me?" cried the outraged leaf, as the wind lifted it high in the air, twisted it this way and that, and blew it up into the clouds over the mountain and away.

"Wait for me!" cried Roger, as he emptied the rest of the bag on himself. Three flakes fell, one on his unkempt head, one on his frayed right elbow, one on the bare toe poking out of his worn left boot. Three flakes weren't much, which may be why it took a full minute and a half for Roger to turn into—a what? If you looked at it from one angle, it was a large, muddy gray, pimply egg. If you looked at it from another angle, it was a rock. From yet another angle, it was a mound of mottled clay. Whatever it was, it wasn't going to blow away in the wind. It wasn't going anywhere. It was stuck forever and a day on the Dastardly Divide.

"No!" cried Roger, from inside the rock or egg or mound of clay. "I'm supposed to be a leaf and blow away with Lady Sadie and find Princess Petulia and slay the giant and rescue her and marry her and bring to an end this awful, endless quest! I can't be whatever I've turned into, which feels like it weighs a thousand pounds and can't move. No! No! No!" Roger was furious. He felt betrayed by his Magic Powder. The enormity of this betrayal made him want to jump up and down in rage and frustration. Except that there was no Roger to jump up and down, only a rock. Or, from another angle, an egg. Or a mound of clay. The egg, rock, or mound of clay jumped.

Not much. How much motion can you expect from a mound of clay, a rock, or an egg? But it moved an inch. Then, an hour later, another inch; then, in twelve more hours, twelve more inches, each inch moving it closer to the edge of the cliff. Because that was where Roger was determined to go. To go over. To fall. To meet his fate, whatever it happened to be. To get to the bottom of it all.

It took three weeks and five days for Roger the Rock—or Egg or Mound of Clay—to reach the edge of the cliff. He teetered there. Below—five hundred feet below—lay a canyon, pencil-thin from his distance, a sliver of a river dab in the middle. Roger did not understand how he knew this. He seemed to be inside and outside the rock or egg or mound of clay at the same time. But he knew exactly where he was. He knew that, with a little more effort, he could tip himself over. And he would fall. He thought, "If I can will myself to the edge, I should be able to will myself where to fall." But his confidence wavered at the thought. How, with all the will in the world, could he land in a river that narrow, that far away, instead of crashing onto the rocks below and shattering into a million pieces? "Because I'm on a quest, that's how," Roger thought.

But this thought was instantly overtaken by another. "What quest?" Roger still wasn't sure of the exact nature of his quest. Was it really to rescue Princess Petulia from the giant? That was a quest, all right, surely *somebody's* quest. But how did he know it was his? Maybe it was Lady Sadie's quest. Did girls have quests? Impossible! Only kings, princes, and knights had quests. And they were on them. And so was Roger, or was he? Which quest? Perhaps turning Lady Sadie into a leaf that was blown off the Dastardly Divide to safety, perhaps that was his quest! Then his quest was over. He could go home now. But how was he to know?

Was rescuing Lady Sadie his quest? Or Princess Petulia? It was like a card trick. Pick a quest, any quest. Don't tell what it is. Now put it back in the deck.

Also, how did he know that Lady Sadie was rescued? Maybe she was lying in a pile of leaves at the bottom of the canyon. She could have been caught in a wind tunnel that spun her hundreds of feet to the foot of the very cliff on top of which Roger teetered indecisively.

The possibility that Lady Sadie needed further rescuing was more than Roger could bear. He had used up all but his last pinch of Magic Powder to get her out of this fix. What if she was not out, but in another fix? Just as he was: Escaping the fix of the Forever Forest to find himself in the fix of the Dastardly Divide. One fix after another. And, after that, were there more fixes waiting out there? A lifetime of fixes, waiting in line. You beat the odds on one only to face the odds on another? And another? And another? And another? And another?

"I'm going to think my-
self into a headache,"
thought Roger, so
rather than think
himself into a
headache (which got
him nowhere), Roger
thought himself over the
edge of the cliff.

•

Which may have been the wrong
thing to do, but at least it
wasn't a headache.

•

His good humor returned as he
fell. The further and faster he
fell, the more convinced he
was that Lady Sadie, the
leaf, lay stranded in the
valley below, waiting
for Roger to come to
her rescue.

•

"Won't she be pleased?" he thought as he crashed at a terrifying speed into a great black boulder a foot short of the riverbank. And broke in two. And out of the broken egg (because that's what it was all along) swooped a baby eagle—Roger!—soaring low on new wings across the valley, checking fallen leaves to see if one of them needed rescuing.

Chapter 13
The Valley of Vengeance

Given the choice, Roger would have preferred to be a man, but he had to admit he led a better life as an eagle. He was the only eagle in the valley. And because of that, he was treated with respect bordering on reverence. He was the most thrilling sight, the only thrilling sight these mean-spirited folk had ever laid eyes on.

For this was the Valley of Vengeance, rich in land, lush in vegetation, and occupied by a gang of truly obnoxious peasants. Greedy, jealous, bad-tempered, always plotting to get even. Get even with whom? It didn't matter. Get even with *anyone*! Farmers and their families woke each morning with a single thought, and it was that same thought that they bedded down with at night. "I've got to get even!" Exactly what they had to get even for was not clear. They were well off, all of them, but perhaps not quite as well off as their neighbor. So they'd get even by burning down their neighbor's house. And he'd burn down theirs in return. So they'd burn down their neighbor's relatives' house. And steal the cattle and chickens and children that went with the house. But by that time someone else, a complete stranger perhaps, was getting even with them.

And that was how the days, months, and years passed in the Valley of Vengeance, until Roger the Eagle made his appearance. When he was fully grown—and he was fully grown in a week—his wingspan cast a shadow that shaded an entire meadow. He could swoop and soar at dizzying speeds, but that's not what he did mostly. What he did mostly was glide inches above the treetops in slow, ever-widening circles.

"He must be searching for something" was the comment made by fighting farmers, who stopped getting even with each other just long enough to watch.

What he was searching for was a talking leaf. Lady Sadie. One moment he was convinced she'd been blown to safety, and the next he was just as certain she was lying at the bottom of a mound of leaves. Ordinary, unenchanted leaves. So he circled over miles of leaves, studying each with his eagle eyes, sifting through them with his eagle talons, whispering so no one but she would hear: "Lady Sadie, is that you? Lady Sadie, is that you?" But she was nowhere that he looked.

She was safe, then. Good. Better than good, wonderful! But Roger was primed for rescue. He was a great eagle of heroic stature. A need to rescue coursed within his veins. If not Lady Sadie, then who? He looked for likely victims. More than enough in the Valley of Vengeance. First of all: children. As farmers, in the act of getting even, dragged off the children and livestock of the farmers with whom they had gotten even, Roger swooped down and plucked the little ones out of the clutches of their captors. Two, three, and four at a time swept away, swept aloft in his powerful talons.

It was enough to strike awe, respect, and second thoughts in the hearts of the mean and greedy. They all but fell to their knees in tribute as Roger robbed them of their prey. Children high in the sky screamed with glee. "Higher! Faster! Dive!" Giddy with flight, they pleaded with Roger to turn their rescues into joyrides. Above the clouds he carried the children, freeing them to fall, to tumble head over heel—and then at the last moment, just before crashing into the trees—a breathtaking swoop, a chilling catch, a riotous rescue. "More! More!" cried the children. The countryside rang with a laughter never before heard in the Valley of Vengeance. Not nasty, not mean, not vengeful, this laughter was merry as spring.

Roger had missed the sound. And now, hearing laughter again, he could not get enough. Particularly this kind. This kind was better than any he had inspired before, because this laughter had a reason.

Laughter is a threat to the vengeful. The mean-spirited dwellers of the valley would have liked to stamp it out. Pass a law. Jail the laughers. Wipe the smiles off their disgusting little faces.

But in the secluded, unpoisoned remains of their hearts, they sensed what was going on. They hated what they sensed, but they sensed it anyway. The laughter overhead made mockery of their disputes. It made them look silly. It made them insignificant. For the first time in their getting-even lives, they felt shame over their grievances.

What could they do but slink away, bewildered and snarling, furious at the happiness that echoed over the countryside?

First furious, then jealous. Why the children, who did nothing to deserve it, and not them? It was unfair. They had to get even with the children. They, too, had to fly!

They came out of hiding, their gnarled hands clasped to their bosoms. "Take us, too!" they demanded of the great eagle. "We protest! We want *our* turn!"

And soon everyone in the valley took a turn. Lifelong enemies, clutched in Roger's talons, grinned foolishly at each other as they sailed heavenward. They looked down on the land over which they fought and got even. They saw, for the first time, that it was—what was the word?—beautiful! Beauty. It was a new idea to them. The image of beauty cut into their hearts like Cupid's arrow.

Day by day, the rage diminished, the need to get even faded, evened out. In a matter of mere weeks, Roger's flights of farmers converted the Valley of Vengeance into the Valley of Very Good Times. Neighbors began saying "Hello," "How are you?" "Nice day!" to each other instead of "Get out of my sight before I walk on your face!"

And all this—every bit of it—was due to Roger. "My goodness," he thought, "how much better I am as an eagle than I was as a prince."

One day he saw two men fighting, or rather one man battering another into helplessness. A rare sight these days. Roger swooped down to put an end to it. Suddenly the husky fellow who was the aggressor turned from his victim and, in a flash, set an arrow to his bow and fired it straight at Roger. Roger was astonished. He barely ducked in time. When the Valley of Vengeance was at its worst—even then!—no one had tried to hurt the noble eagle. He was above the fray. He was special. He was untouchable. But not with this villain.

Roger was upon the assassin seconds before he was ready to get off another shot. He grabbed him by the collar and swooped skyward.

The scoundrel struggled as Roger bore him aloft. Flight did not pacify him. "I'll kill you, you stupid bird! Let me go!" screamed the barbarian, kicking viciously in midair and injuring no one but himself.

Roger had been too busy to take a look at the criminal, but he instantly recognized the voice. "Tom!" This was the first word he had said in a month.

"Roger?" Tom answered in astonishment. "Are you the noble eagle that everyone here worships and who I have sworn to kill?"

Roger was confused. "But, Tom, you swore to me you'd given up hunting!" Thrilled though he was to be reunited with his best friend, Roger was nonetheless deeply disturbed that Tom was out to kill the eagle, who was a far worthier creature than Tom's pal, the prince.

Chapter 14
End of a Friendship

Tom was changed.

Roger was changed too, but if he didn't happen to be an eagle he would have been something like the old Roger. Changed for the better, no doubt about it: a kinder, wiser, stronger Roger. But, still, if you were to run into him on the street outside this book, you'd know him right away. But you wouldn't know Tom. Tom had turned cruel.

Now, as you will recall, I warned you about Tom early on. I told you he wasn't to be trusted. But the old Tom, the Tom I warned you about a while back, was fun to hang out with. There *are* people like that: they're a lot of fun, and you have a fine time with them, and then one day they do something bad. They don't take your side, or they talk about you behind your back, or they steal something that's yours—and you are shocked to discover that, underneath the fun, they are not nice people.

The difference between Tom now and Tom in the old days is that the *old* Tom behaved like a nice person. A friend, a buddy, a pal. But the newly rediscovered Tom behaved like a rat. "I am going to get even," he sneered at Roger when they were back on the ground.

Roger was shocked. "Whatever for?"

"You left me in the Forever Forest. You could have taken me with you, but you didn't. You left me flat. I'm going to get even."

In the old days, before he became an eagle, Roger would have dismissed Tom's complaint as nothing more than his friend in a whiny mood. Tom used to whine a lot and Roger was good at kidding him out of it. He never gave Tom's complaints a second thought.

But the eagle Roger understood what the prince Roger would have laughed at. Tom's point was well taken. Roger felt pangs of guilt. He *hadn't* thought of taking Tom with him when he backed out of the Forever Forest. He hadn't thought of anything except that his bag of Magic Powder was half empty and that he must get out before it was gone. "I was wrong, Tom," Roger said sadly. "I'm sorry."

"I'm going to get even."

"I apologize."

"Someday in some way, when you least expect it, I will get even."

"Look, I said I'm sorry. I said I apologize. I didn't mean anything by leaving you flat. I was just stupid. I forgot. I was wrong. I was stupid. I forgot." Roger went on explaining and apologizing and defending himself until he was blue in the beak. Nothing he did placated Tom.

"Someday when you're asleep or when your back is turned or when your mind is on your stupid quest, I'll get even."

Roger refused to believe that this, his first and only true friendship, could end so badly. It didn't seem sad so much as dumb. Okay, he made a mistake, he acted selfishly. But that was long ago, and he wouldn't act that way today, and he had apologized till he was blue in the beak, so why in the world wouldn't Tom forgive him? What was the problem?

The problem was that Tom was just plain mean. And getting meaner. He was so mean that no matter how many times Roger asked—twenty-five, as a matter of fact—he refused point-blank to explain how he'd escaped from the Forever Forest.

But that doesn't mean I can't tell you.

He walked out. Not out of the forest, out of the book. He left just the way I wanted him to on page 12, but he wouldn't. As you know, he wasn't meant to be in the book past page 12, so he could leave any time he chose. When Roger was no longer available to run and play with, Tom got mad and left.

Not right away. He sulked first, he whined, he whined and sulked, and sulked and whined. He said wicked things about Roger to Large Lucille and the rest of their friends. Things like: "Who told us he would tell me when it was all right and I would tell you when it was all right and I would know right after he would know and then you would know it's all right?—and he didn't mean a word of it!"

But Roger had given them all such pleasure that no one, except Tom, could be mad or blame him for anything, even

if he was at fault. They preferred to think he was playing.

"Roger!" they called. "Where are you hiding, Roger? Come out, come out, wherever you are!" And the loudest caller of all was Large Lucille. This was ironic and pathetic because "Come out, come out, wherever you are!" was exactly what her fiancé, Andrew, had been crying in towns, villages, and hamlets on five continents for thirty years.

Roger's friends could not, would not, believe that he had found a way out of the Forever Forest without taking them with him. But Tom would not stop hammering home the message. He insinuated sly, sneaky, sarcastic, sneering, and, eventually, savage wisecracks. In less time than it takes to write it, Tom went from being Roger's best friend to being his worst enemy.

True, Roger had acted impulsively. But how could he know that walking backward would work? And when it did work, where did it get him? Off the edge of a cliff onto the Dastardly Divide. So did he deserve such treatment from Tom? Certainly not! First of all, princes in fairy tales aren't expected to rescue *everyone* they come in contact with. They are only expected to rescue the main people: princesses, kings, queens, dukes. Nobility. I mean, they're off on a quest, for crying out loud! But whatever was expected of princes in other fairy tales, in this one Roger was made to feel terrible. The more he thought about Tom's accusations, the more he came around to his view that he, Roger, had betrayed his friends of the Forever Forest. Tom was out, he was safe, but the others . . . It brought tears to Roger's eyes to think of them: wandering in circles forever in the Forever Forest. Late as he was, how dare he not fly to the rescue?

Chapter 15
A Further Explanation

I have to put off the part where Roger flies to the rescue because I've left an important question unanswered. Once Tom walked out of the book, how and why did he come back? The answer to that question is: boredom. It's not much of a life for a character in a book to be out of the book. Falling into rosebushes was more fun than what Tom went through out of the book. He went through nothing. Time passed as if it didn't: a second seemed like a month, a minute like a year, an hour like a century.

After several hours that felt like centuries, Tom realized that he had to go back into a book, but he was too angry with Roger to return to this book. So he tried other books. He went into a book called *Charlotte's Web*, but found it too kind and gentle for a man of his mean temperament. He admired the pictures and left. He went into a book called *James and the Giant Peach*. But he found that book to be meaner than he was. So he glanced at the pictures, which he liked, and left. He tried a book called *The Phantom Tollbooth*, but the story was so smart it gave him a headache and the pictures were so loosely drawn that he thought that even he could do better. So he left. And concluded what he should have known in the first place. Only one book was right. This one. So he walked back in. And found himself in "The Valley of Vengeance" chapter. And just as he was beginning to get even by beating people up, Roger came along and stopped him. And that's where we are now.

Chapter 16

Back to the Dastardly Divide

Before he could fly to the rescue, something had to be done about Tom. If Roger flew off and left Tom alone, he'd beat people up. And those people would have to get even. So *they* would beat people up, who'd have to get even. And before long the Valley of Very Good Times would turn back into the Valley of Vengeance. Not a good idea. Tom had to go.

But where? Roger couldn't take him along on the rescue because Tom, no doubt, would try to get even, leaving Roger no choice but to keep a sharp eye on him. And another eye on the Forever Forest. And another eye out for the friends he had come to rescue. He didn't have enough eyes for this job. Not with Tom along. Roger could rescue his friends or he could defend himself, but he couldn't do both.

"Where are you taking me?" Tom demanded to know. And this was understandable since he was in Roger's talons, two hundred feet in the air.

"I'm looking for a place I can put you where you can't do any harm."

"But I *want* to do harm. Doing harm is the best part of getting even," protested Tom.

It was that sort of remark that made Roger decide that the only place he could leave Tom without fear of the consequences was the Dastardly Divide. He foraged about for a supply of food and water that would last Tom until he was able to get back to him. He bound the supplies tightly in a shawl, and then, carrying Tom in his talons and the shawl in his beak, flew up, up, up to the highest cliff of the Dastardly Divide, the very one that he'd backed off months ago. He plopped Tom gently down. "Don't be scared," he said. "I'll zip off to the Forever Forest to rescue our friends, and after that I'll zip right back to rescue you, and after that, if you'll be my friend again, we can zip off to rescue the beautiful princess who turns men to stone from an evil giant, and after that I'll have to marry her, because as far as I can tell, that's my quest."

Roger said all of this in a breathless rush, so eager was he to restore himself to Tom's good graces. But no such luck. Tom's terse response was "I hope the giant squashes you like a bug."

Roger flew away, circling once to make sure that Tom was all right. Tom appeared to be fine. He acted as if he didn't have a care in the world. The last Roger saw of him, he was settling down to a good lunch on the Dastardly Divide.

Of course, Tom knew what Roger didn't. He could get

off the Dastardly Divide any time he liked. After lunch, for instance. All he had to do was walk out of the book. And walk back in and out and in and out and in and out and in as often as he must, until he arrived at the right spot in the story for him to get even.

Chapter 17

Across the Sea of Screams and into the Mountain of Malice

Roger flew backward. He knew no other method of reaching his destination. He flew backward through heavy rain, dense fog, thunderstorms, and blizzards. He flew backward over the Sea of Screams, which was one of the awful places J. Wellington Wizard warned he must pass on his quest. Fearful cries of "Help!" rose up at him from the green-black sea, whose churning waves looked like they were writhing in torture. Roger started down, his eagle eyes skimming the sea's surface. He was there to help, but saw no one who needed help. Whitecaps spattered like outstretched hands pleading for rescue. The screams came with desperate urgency. "Who's screaming?" Roger wondered. Were the waves screaming? Did waves need his help? Roger dipped lower for a better look. A green-black wave unwound like a serpent and coiled around his legs.

Roger pumped his wings and pumped again and broke free. The sea screams turned to whimpers. Sobs of "Help!" Moans of "Help!" But who exactly was Roger to help? The roiling, broiling, stained-dark sea gnashed its waves like teeth.

"You cry 'Help,' but you don't mean 'Help.' You mean you want to swallow me!" Roger screamed back at the Sea of Screams and flew away backward. If he couldn't trust cries of help, if cries of help could swallow and drown him . . . Roger's sense of right and wrong felt dishonored. If this was meant to be a lesson, he didn't want to learn it.

He flew backward across the Mountain of Malice, another of the wicked places J. Wellington had warned him about. Stones flew up at him, grazing his feathers. Who was throwing them? No one. The mountain itself was throwing them. Small boulders zoomed up at Roger with the velocity of cannon shots.

The first rocks didn't come close; but then, as if the mountain had adjusted for Roger's height and speed, they narrowed the distance. Rocks started bouncing off Roger, his head, his chest, his wings. Big and fast though they

were, they stung more than they bruised. Smaller rocks bounced off him harmlessly. But thirty or forty rocks bouncing harmlessly off an eagle in a span of five minutes can do real harm. Roger's pace slowed. He grew dizzy. But it would be fatal to surrender to his dizziness.

He altered his flight pattern in an attempt to confuse the mountain. He flew in circles, high, low, forward, and backward again. He swooped and soared, glided and shot straight up. His strength was returning—and, at the same time, the mountain appeared confused. The velocity of the rocks weakened. As battered as Roger was, now he had no trouble evading the flying missiles. He noticed something different. A barrage of rocks came up at him with notes attached.

Why notes? Roger could not help but be curious. Were these messages? Were they for him? Or for any bird who happened over? Through practice, Roger became adept at darting his beak forward and picking the notes off the rocks. Not all, there were too many, but soon he held an untidy collection crumpled in his talons.

Night was coming on. Roger was less clear a target now. The barrage wavered, hesitated, stopped. Roger plucked one last note off one last rock and flew backward onward, out of the reach and soon out of sight of the Mountain of Malice.

He hurt all over. He needed to rest, to eat, to sleep. But before anything else, he needed to read the notes. He found himself within sight of a farm. In the distance, he saw the lights of a neighboring village, but Roger was too exhausted to investigate. He headed for the roof of an old barn and set himself down.

His weary eyes took in acres of land, ripe to feast on. But later, he thought, after he read the notes. First the notes, then a hearty meal (a pumpkin patch lay directly below, and to the east, row upon row of corn). Following his feast, he would have a good night's rest. No sooner had Roger fixed this schedule in his mind than he changed it entirely by falling asleep.

He awoke to the cry of roosters. Dawn was rising, probably in the east—but Roger was so bruised and confused that, for all he knew, dawn could have risen in the north, south, or west. He discovered a brook nearby and bathed his wounds and bruises while snapping down a sampling of trout and bass. He was beginning to feel like himself again—that is, his noble eagle self. He was battered but not seriously hurt. He was convinced that his pain would be gone in a few hours. He remembered the notes. He flew back to the roof of the barn, uncrumpled and read them. His pain returned. Worse than before. Worse than anything he had endured.

It would be needlessly cruel to print all of the notes, but here's a sample:

"YOU ARE A VAIN AND SELFISH LOUT."

"YOU CAN'T HOLD ON TO YOUR FRIENDS."

"YOU CANNOT BELIEVE THE AWFUL THINGS THEY ARE SAYING ABOUT YOU IN THE FOREVER FOREST." "THEY DESPISE YOU."

"THEY WILL TEAR YOU TO PIECES WHEN THEY SEE YOU." "YOU ARE MORE OF A LAUGHING-STOCK NOW THAN WHEN YOU WERE A PRINCE."

"LADY SADIE IS DEAD, AND IT'S YOUR FAULT."

"PRINCESS PETULIA WAS RESCUED WEEKS AGO BY A BRAVE KNIGHT. THEY ARE LIVING HAPPILY EVER AFTER." "YOUR QUEST IS A DISASTER."

"TOM WILL KILL YOU."

At last, Roger understood how the Mountain of Malice had come by its name. The wounds inflicted by the notes hurt worse than the rocks. Each one contained a crushing truth. Certainly, they had the ring of truth. Roger believed them to be true. Rocks don't lie.

He sat atop the barn, all his will to rescue fading. All his will to continue his quest or, for that matter, his life fading. Nothing was worth this torment. If he were still a prince, he would have wept. Eagles may not be able to weep, but they can brood. In the history of eagledom, no eagle brooded as did Roger during the seven days and nights that followed. He did not eat or sleep, he brooded. He had suffered a mortal wound from the Mountain of Malice. All he wished for now was for his misery to be at an end. He perched, shrunken and hunched, atop the roof of the barn, half-dozing, half-dying. The farm birds and

animals steered clear, out of respect for his condition. Cows slept in the fields at night, birds diverted their flight paths to avoid going over the barn.

Nine full days of this, and on the tenth morning his blurred vision spotted a man. The first being of any sort he had seen since he had taken to his perch to die. Roger was too weak to see clearly, but his hearing remained sharp. Although the man was a quarter mile away, Roger had no difficulty making out his shout, repeated again and again as he came closer.

It was: "Come out, come out, wherever you are! Lucille! Come out, come out, wherever you are!"

Chapter 18

Andrew

First of all, Andrew was surprised that the big, dead-looking bird on the barn roof was alive. Second, he was shocked when it spoke to him. Third, he was stunned when the first word it spoke—shaky but unmistakable—was "Andrew?"

"Andrew?" the all-but-dead eagle wheezed again.

"I must be hearing the death cry of an eagle, which, coincidentally, happens to sound like my name, but probably goes more like, 'Adrooo, andoo, adooo . . .'" That was how Andrew explained the croaking sounds coming out of the close-to-gone bird. Not an unreasonable explanation, considering that he had never met or heard of Roger. But how was he to explain what followed?

"Aren't . . . you . . . Lucille's . . . Andrew?"

Under ordinary circumstances, Andrew might have been expected to faint dead away, or run off as fast as his rubbery legs would carry him. This pale ghost of an eagle had spoken not just *his* name but that of the woman he loved and had been in search of for thirty years.

But the circumstances were far from ordinary. Thirty years without a clue to his lost love's whereabouts, and this bird—who was about to die on him—knew something. He *could* not die—not until he had told all! Andrew, though no longer young, vaulted to the roof of the barn, scooped up the suffering bird in his arms (it was like carrying melted wax), and ran with him to a nearby brook.

Carefully, in fear that a false move would be fatal, Andrew spooned water down the poor eagle's beak, bathed him, fed him a gruel made of rabbit and trout. He spread the poor thing out to dry in the sun, and gently massaged its limp, chilled body that had little more substance than a shadow. He felt signs of warmth. Blood flowing. "You will not die," growled Andrew, gritting his five remaining teeth.

"Yes, I will," wheezed Roger.

But Andrew was determined. "You will not die."

"If you are Andrew, I should not die," conceded Roger, dimly recalling his mission to rescue Lucille and the others from the Forever Forest.

"I *am* Andrew."

"If you are Lucille's Andrew, I cannot die."

"I *am* Lucille's Andrew."

"Then," said Roger, weakly but firmly, "I cannot die, for it now occurs to me that you are my quest."

His recovery was nothing short of magical, which, considering the fact that he was an enchanted prince, was no big deal. By dusk, Roger looked and acted like his heroic eagle self. He filled Andrew in on *everything*: the Forever Forest, Lucille, Tom, his escape from the Forever Forest, Lady Sadie, the Dastardly Divide, the Valley of Vengeance, the Valley of Very Good Times, the Sea of Screams, the Mountain of Malice, his ever-changing, ever-expanding quests.

"But enough about me," said Roger, as the new day dawned. "Tell me about yourself."

But Andrew had no story to tell. Thirty years of search and travel, travel and search. Thirty years from north to south, from east to west. Thirty years of more experience, more adventure, more meetings with more different kinds and colors of people—rich and poor, good and bad, smart and stupid, earnest and lazy, stimulating and boring, honest and wicked, wise and foolish—than even Roger had undergone. A lifetime of spectacular comings and goings. And not a bit of it registered. From none of it did Andrew learn a thing. Nothing was noticed, nothing counted, nothing had meaning without Lucille.

"Take me to her!" pleaded Andrew.

"Better than that, I will bring her to you."

Andrew moaned. "You will fly away and you won't return. And year after year I will knock on door after door crying, 'Come out, come out, wherever you are!'"

"You saved my life, you restored my hope. How can I not return?"

"I don't know how you cannot return, but you won't. In a lifetime of learning nothing from experience, the one lesson I *have* learned is that if you do unto others as you would have others do unto you, they don't."

"I do! I shall! I will!" Suddenly, without warning, Roger spread his wings. They sprang apart with the force of a catapult. The sheer breadth of Roger in good health scared Andrew half to death. Blotted from sight was his entire view, the barn where he'd found the sick bird as well as the brook where he saved his life.

"What are you doing?" he demanded of Roger. A sensible question, because the great eagle had lifted him by the collar and was zipping him back and forth across the meadow at nerve-shattering speed.

"I have to make sure that I am strong enough for the journey. I have miles to go, I don't know how many. I have dozens to rescue, I don't know how many. But if I took you along, I know this: it would be one too many. So stay where you are. Do not knock on any more doors. Cut a swath in this meadow in the shape of a heart. Cut it two acres deep and one acre wide. And that will be the landmark that will guide me back with your Lucille."

Chapter 19
Doveen the Serene

A small village lay a mile from the meadow that Andrew was remaking in the shape of a heart. Villagers, on their daily rounds, were surprised to see the stranger cutting a swath through the overgrown grass and weeds and wild flowers. "Who are you, where are you from, and what are you reaping?" they had to know.

Between strokes of his slashing scythe, Andrew responded: "I am Andrew. I am from far and beyond. What do I reap? Nothing. What shall I harvest? Love. For my lost Lucille, who will be returned to me on the wings of an eagle on the day I turn this meadow into a heart."

A lost love? The wings of an eagle? A meadow turned into a heart? Talk like that was bound to draw a crowd. The village emptied. While no one seriously believed in Andrew's eagle, no one wanted to be absent if and when it happened to land with Lucille. Days and nights Andrew worked as villagers built campsites and lean-tos near the spreading outskirts of the heart. A village sprang out of nowhere, with a marketplace, shops, merchants, vendors, artisans, magicians, jugglers, an inn . . . The noise was deafening.

And on the twelfth day there appeared an authentic sorceress, a fortuneteller who, for a price, forecast the future. Her name was Doveen, and she was known as Doveen the Serene, an island of calm amidst the bustle. She had a crystal ball. She charged a frogett (which would be a nickel in our day) to look into it.

"What do you see, Doveen the Serene?" a villager asked.

"I see trees." Doveen

the Serene did not look old and she did not look young.

"What have trees got to do with the eagle and a lost love?" asked a second villager.

"The eagle is in the trees." Doveen the Serene did not look pretty and she did not look homely.

"What trees?" asked a third villager.

"Far from here, trees and trees and trees and trees." Doveen the Serene did not look like anyone from around there and she did not look like anyone from around anywhere else.

"How far from here?" asked a fourth villager.

"Closer than you think, farther than you imagine." Doveen the Serene did not look tall, although when she stood she was taller than anyone in the village. But she never stood. No one saw her stand or walk or leave her place behind the crystal ball.

"Is the lost love lost among the trees?" asked a fifth villager.

"All are among the trees, but all are not lost loves." Maybe it was her voice, which was low and musical, or maybe it was her manner, which was gentle and yet threatening, or maybe it was her stare, which was unfocused but seemed to miss nothing. Whatever it was, the villagers believed every word Doveen the Serene spoke, although they did not understand anything she said.

"Has this lost love been found?" asked a sixth villager.

"Have *you* been found?" The question struck fear in

the villagers' hearts, they knew not why.

"We are not lost," a seventh villager responded, sounding uncertain.

"Then that is your answer!"

The villagers retired to their encampment, where they spent the rest of the day and night arguing, because no two of them could agree on what Doveen the Serene had told them.

Dawn rose on the thirteenth day. The villagers awakened to see the distant figure of Andrew returning from the far end of the meadow with the scythe balanced on his shoulder. A strange sight: the first time in two weeks that they saw Andrew not cutting grass. Sure enough, his work was done. The two-acre-deep, one-acre-wide heart shone like a prairie fire in the brilliant half-light of early morning.

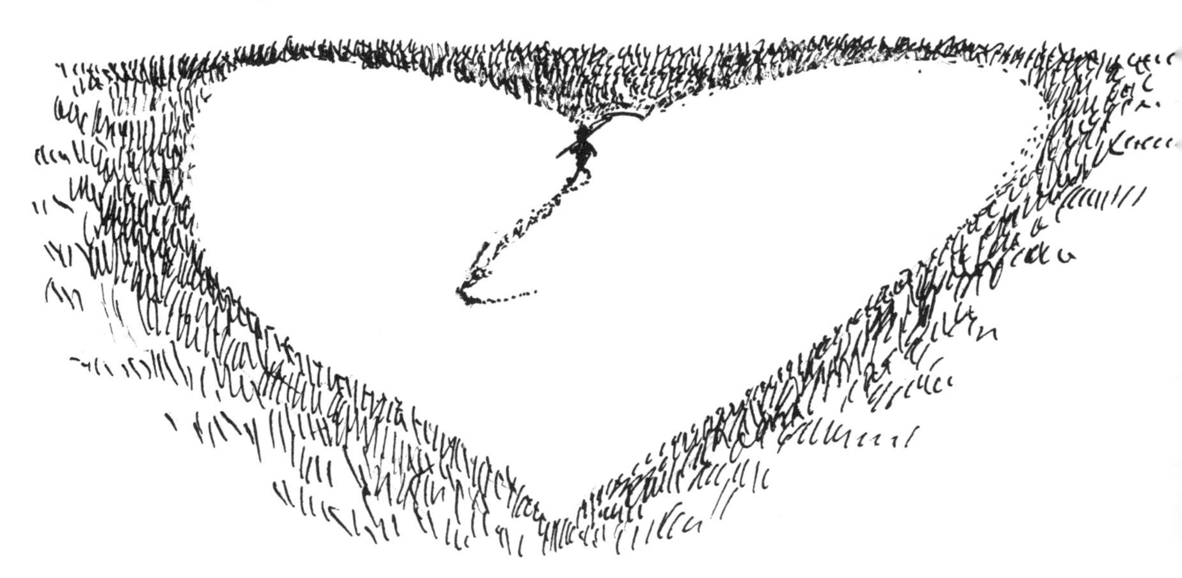

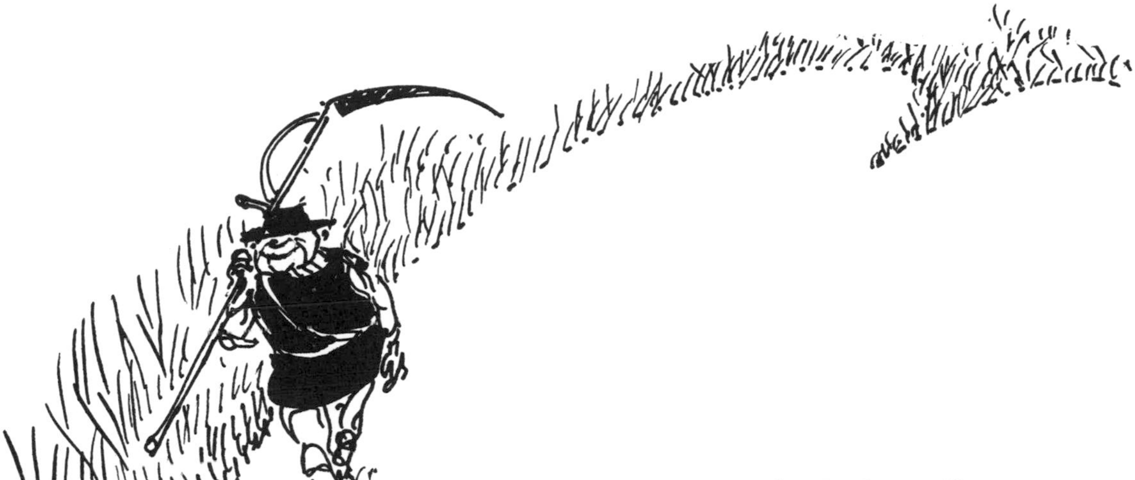

As Andrew approached, the villagers saw that he, too, was aglow. His smile was as bright as the new day. It could have been a smile earned for a job well done. Or it could have been a smile of anticipation. He was facing the wrong direction, so he could not see the black dot moving fast out of the distant rosy-hued clouds. The dot took on size and shape as it came closer. The villagers spotted some kind of bird carrying some kind of burden. But Andrew's back was turned, so that wasn't why he smiled. Only when the villagers returned his smile with whoops and leaps of joy did Andrew look over his shoulder to see what all the fuss was about.

Chapter 20
The Toast

It was as if they had never been apart. Oh yes, there was a first moment of shyness.

"Is that you, Andrew?"

"Is that you, Lucille?"

They had changed. He was thinner and grayer and lined. And she was fat. So fat that Roger had to land five or six times on the flight back to catch his breath and restore his energy. But however the years affected their looks, they had no effect on their feelings. The first moment of awkwardness was followed by tears of wonder and years of bliss.

The years of bliss were preceded by a wedding ceremony performed at the center of the heart by Doveen the Serene, with the entire village in attendance. Roger was nowhere to be seen. Moments after the reunion, he had slunk off to the darkest corner of the farthest edge of the heart-shaped field, an exhausted and confused bird. He was too ashamed to join the wedding. He didn't think he had the right. This celebration was not for him. He heard the music and gaiety from a distance that he felt he could not cover in a lifetime.

What would have happened back there in the Forever Forest if Lucille had discovered his true identity? She would have refused to fly with him. His other friends, too. Roger cringed at the thought. The sounds of the wedding celebration faded from his ears, replaced by memories of his return to the Forever Forest. What cheers! His old friends somehow understood at a glance the mission that this noble-looking eagle, soaring high overhead, had come on. They pranced, they danced, Lucille among them (she was the easiest to spot from Roger's height because of her size).

Roger flew in descending circles, slower and lower, as if he meant to draw an even greater response from them. But this was not the case, just the opposite. The closer he came, the louder their cheers, the more a voice inside him cried: "Flee!"

Roger could barely restrain himself from turning in his descent and flying away. What could he say to these friends he had abandoned? Not for a moment did he doubt the truth of the notes wrapped around the rocks hurled at him by the Mountain of Malice. His friends despised him, so said the rocks. So Roger believed. He had walked out on them. Backward, yes, not knowing where he was going, yes—but still and all, the rocks were right, Tom was right. He should have thought of his friends; he should have taken them with him. How could he fly down now and say, "Hi! Sorry for being late, but better late than never. I've come to your rescue." How could he say that? How could he say anything? He couldn't. He didn't.

Not a word did he speak during the five days and nights it took him to fly his old friends backward out of the Forever Forest. Through blue skies, gray skies, stormy, hazy, and star-lit skies he flew them out, two at a time, one in each talon. None were afraid. No matter the height, no matter the distance, no matter the weather, they trusted the eagle as if he were an old friend, not realizing that he *was* an old friend. "I like this eagle," Roger heard Tim the Troubadour sing out. "Oh, don't you wish Roger was here to enjoy this?"

He was amazed at how often Roger, the prince's name, came up in the course of the flights. "Roger is not going to believe this."

"We must remember every detail to tell Roger if we're lucky enough to meet him again."

"I bet Roger would make the noble eagle laugh so hard he'd drop him."

After hearing such remarks, did it occur to Roger that his friends *didn't* hate him, that the rocks had lied? Not at all. He had been through too much; he found it easier to accept a vile lie wrapped around a rock than a sweet truth spoken by a friend.

So he took not an ounce of pleasure in his mission. Rather, he suffered greatly. Here were his friends chattering cheerfully about him, not dreaming that the prince they praised was the eagle who was flying them to safety. "First I desert them, and now I fool them. Oh, I am the most monstrous of creatures," thought Roger. "Small wonder they hate me."

The tender words his friends used were turned by Roger against himself. With each trip out of the Forever Forest, he managed to change praise into reproach. He had made himself into his own rock, injuring himself with his own bitter notes.

He released his friends, who he knew hated him, on the outer edge of the woods, depositing them on roads that went in one direction only: away from the Forever Forest. Large Lucille he saved for last, because she had the furthest to go.

Roger did not take notice that the wedding celebration, which had been going on riotously all night, had quieted down for the toasts. Mugs, goblets, and tankards of mead, wine, and ale were raised in tribute to Andrew and Lucille. From the length and affection of the toasts, it would have been hard to guess that just a few days earlier no one had heard of the happy couple. And then, with signs of a new dawn, the first since the sighting of the eagle and Lucille, Andrew was called upon to make his toast. He stood at the center of the heart in the field. He raised his mug high. "I lost my bride, I lost my faith, I lost my way. I found an eagle. And the eagle brought back to me all that I lost. To my friend, to my benefactor, to my eagle!"

The crowd cheered, then hushed. It was Lucille's turn. The early rays of dawn glared off her raised goblet. "Though I am twice his size and seven or eight times his weight, the steadfast eagle carried me like a babe into the tender arms of my beloved. I thank him, but that is not enough. I wonder at him, but that is not enough. I toast him, but that is not enough."

"The eagle! Bring on the eagle!" cried the crowd.

But no one had seen the eagle all night. The hero of the celebration had been forgotten by the celebrators. Roger was lying out of sight in the darkest corner of the farthest edge of the heart-shaped field. He lay hunched like a rock, one of the rocks he had been throwing at himself. He didn't have the heart to join the party. He didn't have the will to sneak away. Exhausted by the flight, the rescue, and the rocks he threw at himself, he lay lost in the night, only dimly aware that Doveen the Serene had signaled that it was her turn to toast.

No one actually saw her signal. No one saw her make a move, but nonetheless all eyes were on her. Roger's, too. Half-hooded, his eyes took her in. Doveen the Serene raised a goblet. Her voice was little more than a whisper, but it wafted like the wind across the darkened field to the rocklike Roger. "I wish to toast the two who are one."

The villagers cheered. For once they understood Doveen; she meant Andrew and Lucille. Doveen the Serene's face broke into the smallest trace of a smile. The smile was another signal. It quieted the crowd. "Lastly," she said, "I wish to toast one who is not himself but someone else. On a quest that is neither here nor there. Born a barrel of laughs, drowned in a vale of tears. Once good for nothing but didn't care, now good for everything but doesn't know. To Roger," Doveen said softly.

"To Roger!" thundered the villagers, passionately crying out a name none of them had ever heard before.

In the darkest recess of the heart-shaped field, Roger shuddered. A great weight, heavy as all the rocks thrown at him, rose through his body with the sudden lightness of a cloud. It ruffled his feathers, it bristled his wings. He could not breathe. He opened his beak. The cloud poured out. The weight lifted. Roger lifted. He was aloft. Not on an errand or a mission or a quest. He was aloft because he was weightless now. His body would not stay grounded. It zipped back and forth over the heart-shaped field, climbing, plunging, soaring, looping the loop. Where Roger had not heard his old friends, he had heard Doveen. Somehow, she had gotten through to him. What she had said, what she had left unsaid. Her toast sounded inside Roger with the tremor of a church organ. His spirits soared. And because he was still an eagle, when his spirits soared, so did he.

Chapter 21

Wait

That night, following another day of celebration, Roger slowly descended (his first landing in twelve hours) to visit Doveen the Serene. "Before I leave, I wanted to thank you."

She was not surprised to hear the eagle speak. Nothing surprised her. She was serene.

"You alone know who I am," said Roger.

"I know, but do you know?" answered Doveen in that way she had, where she seemed to say a lot but nobody knew what it was.

"I was born a barrel of laughs. I understand that part. And then you said, 'drowned in a vale of tears.' But I'm *not*. You freed me. I'm soaring, not drowning." Roger's eyes peered deeply into Doveen's. She said nothing. She only smiled. "I'm not drowning, and I'm not in a vale of tears. All I'm asking for is an explanation."

Doveen smiled serenely. "Wait."

Roger shook his head impatiently. "What about Lady Sadie?"

Doveen smiled serenely. "Wait."

"How can I wait, when I don't know if she's alive or

dead? The rocks said she was dead!"

"Wait," said Doveen the Serene.

"Wait? I don't mean to be rude, but all you say is 'Wait.' I waited three years in the Forever Forest. I don't see how waiting any more will help," sputtered Roger in confusion.

Doveen the Serene smiled serenely. "What is Lady Sadie?"

Roger didn't know what to say. "What do you mean, what is she? Lady Sadie is— She's a lady— She's a lady—" He stopped, with his beak wide open. Nothing else came out.

"A lady? What kind of lady?" It was as if Doveen was giving him a test.

"She's a Lady Sadie . . . she's a . . . a . . ." Roger pondered. He never did well on tests; as a prince, he didn't have to. "She's a lady-in-waiting!" he finally cried in exasperation.

"And what do ladies-in-waiting do?" Doveen asked serenely.

It was almost too much for Roger. If eagles could perspire, he would have. His eagle brow furrowed as he paused for a long time.

"They wait?" he asked uncertainly. "Ladies-in-waiting wait?"

Doveen the Serene nodded serenely.

"You mean Lady Sadie is waiting?" Roger asked with rising excitement. "Lady Sadie is alive . . . and waiting?" Roger was startled by his own reaction. Why was he atingle? Certainly, he liked Lady Sadie. But he liked everybody, so why should he be overcome with delight to hear that Lady Sadie was waiting? Not wishing to go into this further, he changed the subject. "Princess Petulia? Is she rescued from the giant? Is she wed, as the rocks said?"

"She waits," said Doveen the Serene.

"Princess Petulia waits?"

"She waits," said Doveen the Serene.

"Princess Petulia waits and Lady Sadie waits?"

Doveen the Serene smiled serenely.

"Everyone waits? What about my friend Tom?"

"He waits."

"He waits. She waits. They wait." Roger sighed. "I'm not at all sure that your answers help me."

Doveen the Serene gave Roger her most serene smile. "Wait," she said.

Chapter 22
The Change

Roger the Eagle flew over a shimmering-silver moonlit sea. He sensed—what did he sense?—so many things. He sensed peace of mind. All he had to do was wait . . . and he would find Lady Sadie . . . and he would meet Princess Petulia. He sensed a new zest for the quest. Whatever and wherever it was, he had only to wait until he faced the unknown challenge that was to be the making of him. And then his journey would be over. And his life as an eagle? Sooner or later, that too would be over. In a way, how sad: He had been an excellent eagle. Could he be so excellent a man? How much harder could that be?

He felt—there is no other word for it—serene as he flew back to the Dastardly Divide. "Wait till I rescue Tom. He must think I forgot him. I'll bet anything he'll forgive me and we'll be the best of friends again." This sweet dream of friendship made Roger fly higher and faster, racing the moon above the bright silver sea. "Wait till Tom and I rescue Lady Sadie," Roger thought serenely. "Wait till I rescue Princess Petulia." There was no end of exciting waiting to be done, and it all lay ahead. The many things he was prepared to wait for unrolled before him like a golden stairway rising to the moon, dipping to the sea. "Oh, I can hardly wait!" Roger thought to himself, his heart melting with a mixture of serenity and joy.

Just about then, he noticed that he was losing altitude. Something had gone wrong with his wings. He turned his eagle's head to look.

Uh-oh. His wings were losing feathers; they were turning back into arms.

"Wouldn't you know it?" sighed Roger, the former eagle, as he plunged into the sea.

Chapter 23

The Vale of Tears

Somebody was kissing him. Why was he spitting water at her when she was nice enough to kiss him? A stranger. She kissed him. Water streamed out of his mouth. She kissed him. Water streamed out of his nose. She kissed him. He remembered he was supposed to be doing something. What was it? Something besides spitting up water.

"Breathe," a soft voice said.

Ah! That was it! Breathe! But how could he breathe if this strange woman, who had him cradled in her arms, insisted on bending over and kissing him? Somehow, in spite of her, he began to breathe. He began to cough. He coughed for a long time.

"Breathe," she insisted.

It was easy for her to say, not so easy for him to do. It took a minute, but he learned to breathe and cough at the same time. And gasp as well. Breathe, cough, gasp. A little of that can go a long way, and then he felt almost ready to be alive again. He looked up from the lap that held him into the face that saved him. The face was so beautiful it took his breath away. He could not afford to have his breath taken away. He started to gasp and cough again. "What do you call that?" were Roger's first words to the beautiful stranger.

"What do I call what?"

"What were you doing, that kissing stuff?"

"That is called the Kiss of Life. I apologize for doing it before we were properly introduced."

"I would have drowned."

"You fell into the sea. Right over there." She pointed to a spot about a half mile away. Roger noticed a trail of floating feathers.

"How did you rescue me?"

"I swam. How else was I to rescue you?"

Roger had no idea where he was. He appeared to be on a large raft of some kind. But the raft had on a shirt and pants. "You swam from here all the way over there?" He looked at the beautiful woman. She was rather small.

"I am an excellent swimmer," she said quietly.

"Then you swam back with me? And pulled me up on this raft? And gave me the Kiss of Life?"

"You would have done the same for me."

"I couldn't, I can't swim. Besides, I'm the one who's on the quest. I'm supposed to do the rescuing." Roger sounded peevish.

"I'm sure you've done more than your share of rescuing."

"And every time I'm rescued it's by a girl." The realization annoyed him. "First Lady Sadie, now you."

The beautiful woman beamed at the mention of Lady Sadie. "You must be Prince Roger, Lady Sadie is my lady-in-waiting, I am Princess Petulia!"

Princess Petulia gave Roger a smile of paralyzing dazzle. But Roger was too interested in the fate of Lady Sadie to notice. "Is Lady Sadie alive?"

"Oh, yes."

"Is she well?"

"She is well."

"Where is she?" Roger looked around. He saw no sign of Lady Sadie.

"She is kidnapped."

"I thought *you* were kidnapped."

"I *am* kidnapped."

"Where is your kidnapper?" Roger looked around.

"You are sitting on him. I am sitting on him, poor dear. This raft is my kidnapper."

Roger tried to get to his feet, but stumbled. Princess Petulia extended her hand, but he was too proud to accept any more of her help. He managed to rise, shakily and slowly, all by himself. He was amazed to see that he was standing five buttons down the shirt of a floating dead giant.

"Is this the giant who kidnapped you?"

"It's a long story," said Princess Petulia, who was also on her feet, positioning herself to catch Roger in case he fell.

"Is he dead?" Roger asked.

"It's a long story."

"Is Lady Sadie in the story?" Otherwise, Roger didn't want to hear it.

"She has a very important part."

"Then I'll listen," said Roger, collapsing into a sprawl on the floating dead—or not so dead—giant.

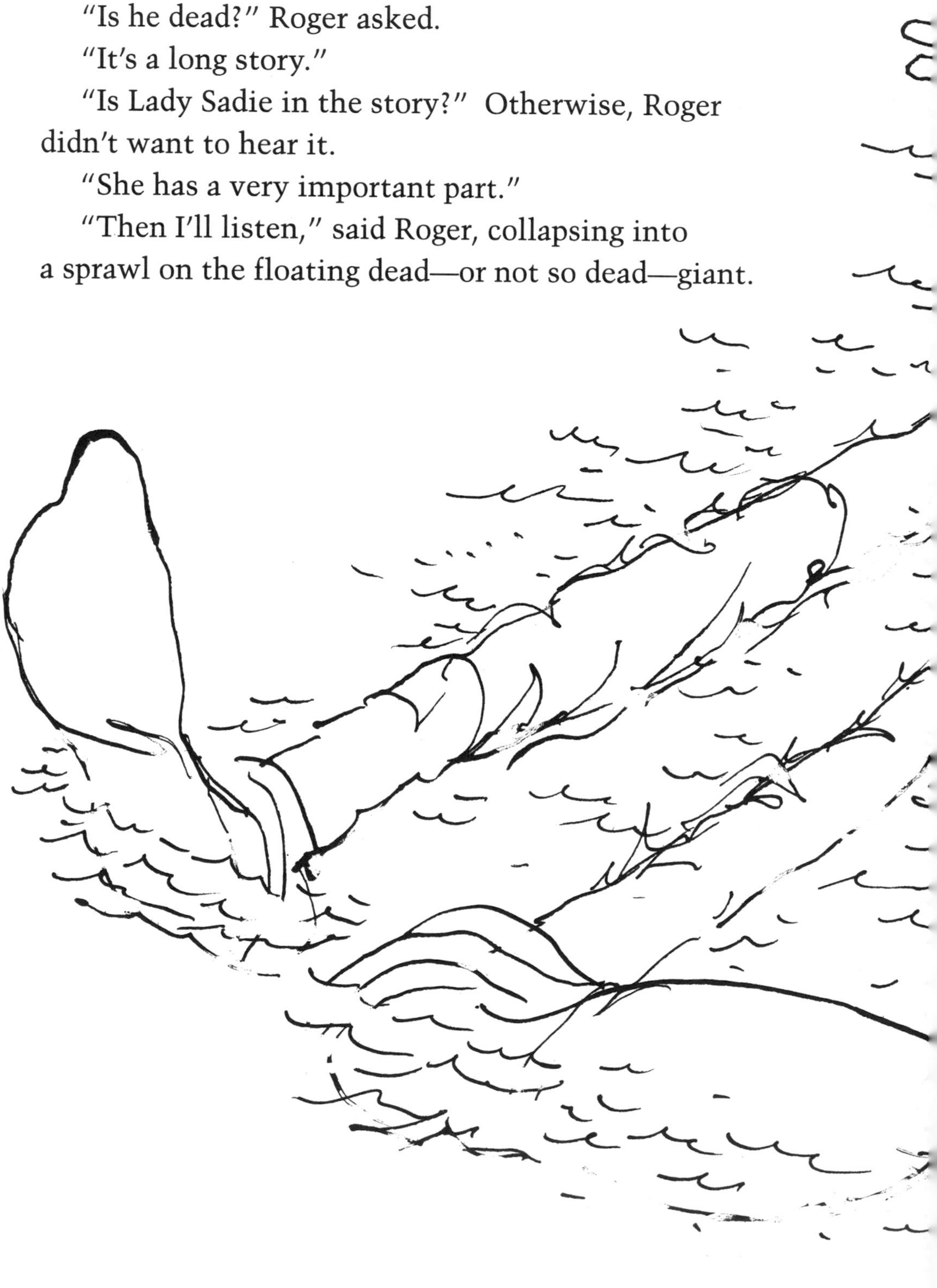

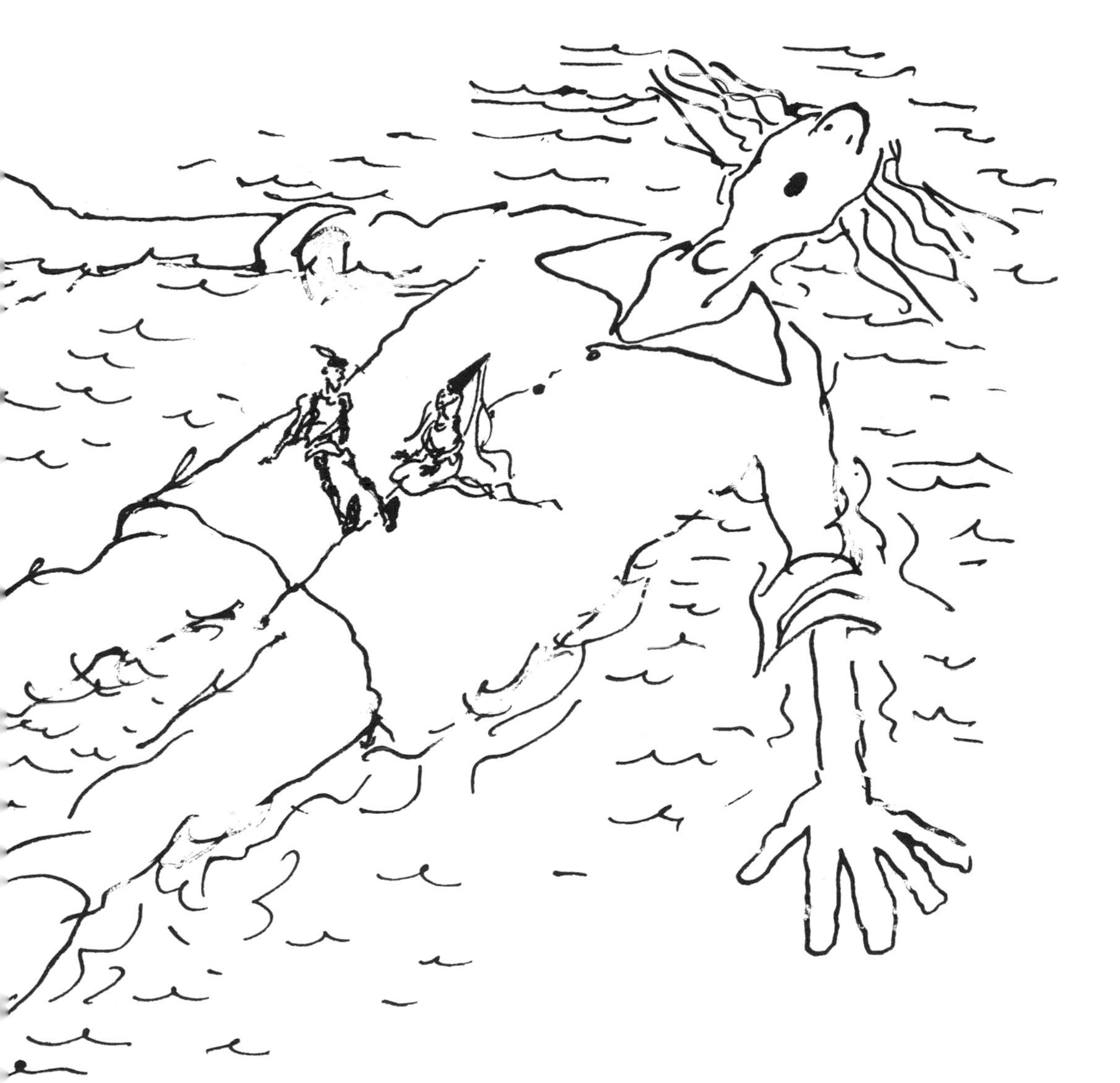

Before beginning her story, Princess Petulia slipped her veil back into place. It was a dark net of spun gold so thick that it was hard to be sure a face was behind it. "Forgive me, but I have been wearing a veil for so long that I am uncomfortable without it. I removed it only to give you the Kiss of Life. You are the first man since my birth to see me full in the face without turning to stone. However, if you were to keep looking at me—" She hesitated. "It's better not to tempt fate."

She could not help but notice that Roger looked puzzled. "Don't you find me astonishingly—even paralyzingly—beautiful?"

Roger frowned. "Now? Or before?"

"You can't see me now. I meant before."

"Look, I'm not going to turn to stone, if that's what worries you."

"Am I losing my looks?" Princess Petulia sounded pleased.

"I don't want to hurt your feelings or anything—"

"Please, be frank."

Roger wished he could find a gentler way of putting it. "You're the most beautiful woman I've ever seen, but . . . you're older than I am, aren't you?"

Roger felt a distinct chill in the air. A silence followed the chill. The chill and the silence went on for a while—far too long, Roger thought—before Princess Petulia sighed and began her story.

"I was blessed with a beauty so astonishing that from the time of my birth my blessing has been my curse. The royal physician who delivered me took one look and said, 'It's a beautiful g—' and he turned to stone. The first boy to become my playmate—I was three—the Duke of Dropsy, teasingly lifted the veil imposed on me since birth. *He* turned to stone. The queen, my mother, did not think my new teeth were coming in straight. She sent for the royal dentist. He begged not to examine me. 'Examine her teeth only, and you will come to no harm,' my mother assured him. A hood was placed over every part of my face but my mouth. The dentist finished his examination, and my mother was right: no harm came to him. The poor fellow was overcome with a sense of smugness. He said to me, 'Now, little princess, that didn't hurt, did it? Give your kindly friend, the royal dentist, a big smile.' I smiled. My smile is astonishingly beautiful. The dentist turned to stone.

"When I came of age, the king, my father, offered a fortune in gold and my hand in marriage to any suitor of noble birth who looked into my face without turning to stone. Suitors of royal blood traveled from the four corners of the earth to accept the challenge. All of them were young, handsome, strong, and brave. All of them are stone. Year after year it went. And you are right, I am no spring chicken—but I remain no less beautiful. Hundreds of stone statues ring our palace walls, each leaning forward with an arm extended. Their thumbs and forefingers are joined, frozen for all eternity in the gesture of lifting a veil.

"Did I grieve for these stone suitors of mine? No. How could I? They had all failed me. My heart hardened toward them. It turned to stone.

"And so it was, until the giant came. He was not noble. But he was big. The size of three tall oaks standing one atop the other. The news of my astonishing beauty had reached him in his wanderings. And wander was what he did, poor soul. His size inspired fear and hatred. He was driven from one land to another, unable to eat or drink in peace. He became frail. He took ill. He tripped. Often. He crushed everything beneath him when he fell. Entire towns. Entire forests.

"He spent more time falling than standing. He came to be sneered at. His name is Philip, but his enemies renamed him Flop. Flop, the falling giant. In his feverish state, he came to believe that if he rescued me he would be loved. He was convinced that he could look upon me in safety because the distance between his head and mine when he lifted my veil would be an eighth of a mile.

"But he is not of royal blood. He well understood that the king, my father, would send his armies to slay him before he was allowed to penetrate the palace walls. So he knew that he must keep his plan a secret.

"It was a simple plan. One morning he would step over the palace walls and kidnap me. Carry me off so fast and so far that my father's horses would never find him.

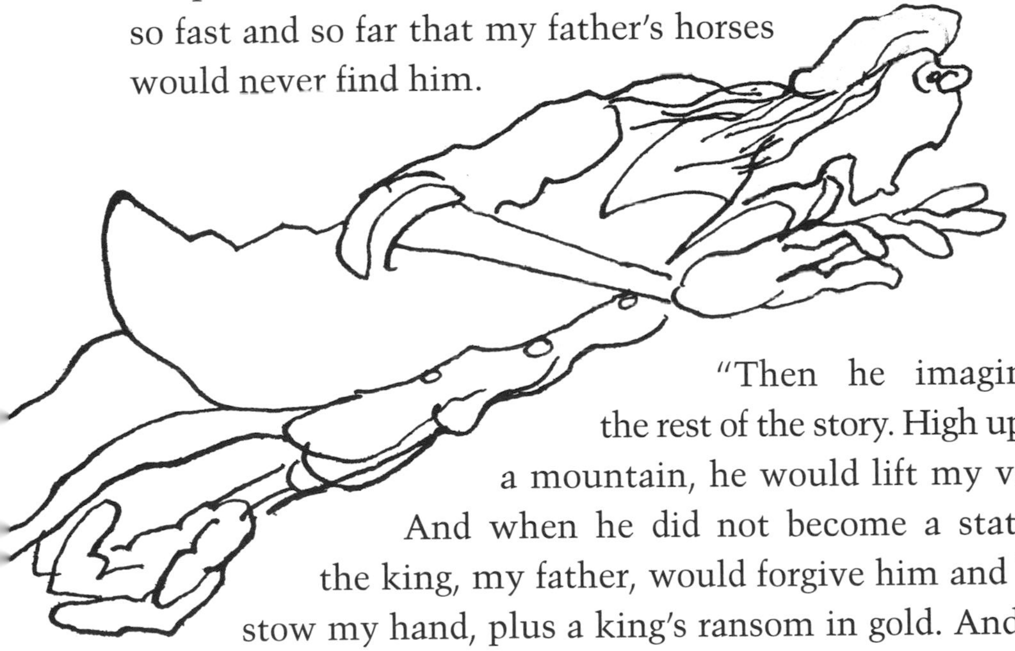

"Then he imagined the rest of the story. High upon a mountain, he would lift my veil. And when he did not become a statue, the king, my father, would forgive him and bestow my hand, plus a king's ransom in gold. And so the giant and I would be wed.

"That was his secret, but not much of one, because Philip, as I call him, and Flop, as others call him, talks to himself. He has no one else to talk to. And since he is as tall as three oaks, one atop the other, his voice carries vast distances. It carried to my father's royal guard, who prepared themselves to kill Philip the moment he set foot within the kingdom.

"Word reached me of the plot to kill the giant

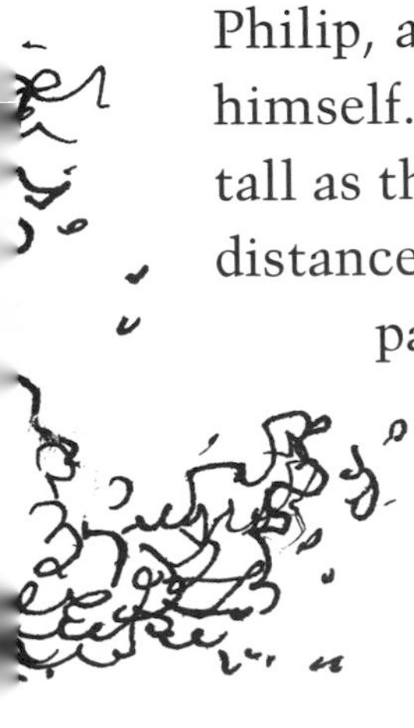

who plotted to kidnap me. For no reason that I can fathom, I wished that the giant be given the opportunity shared by the seven hundred statues that circle the palace walls. 'Let him lift my veil!' I beseeched the king, my father. Alas, he no longer listens to me, and why should he? I am a great disappointment. I am an astonishing beauty who has not once given the king and queen, my parents, a moment's peace or pleasure. My father dismissed my pleas. Flop the Giant was to be slain.

"Why should this have meant anything to a princess with a heart of stone? The answer can only be that I am peculiar. Princess Petulia the Peculiar. I kidnapped myself.

"I fled the palace weeks before the giant's expected arrival. I went in search of him. He was not hard to find. I just followed the sound of a voice telling secrets. It took many miles over many days, but at last I found him. He was lying on his back in a shallow mountain stream. He had fallen a few days before and was too weak to get up. He looked terribly ill. But dear, very dear. I was moved to help. Yes, my stone heart was moved. What caused it to move, why I allowed it to move—these questions I ask myself to this moment and have no answers. I tried to help him rise. I couldn't. He was too big. I tried to find food for him. I can fish; the king, my father, taught me to fish. But the few guppies that I fished out of the stream were no more than a nibble to the giant. Nothing I could do was going to save him.

"I am a princess. I come from a powerful kingdom. I am powerful myself. I can turn men to stone, but I could not turn the shallow stream in which the giant lay dying into a river full of fish that would keep him alive. I wept. It was my first time. I have caused tears in others, hundreds of others, but had not felt the salt of a tear running down my own cheek. I did not know why I wept. Out of helplessness? Out of rage? I wept and I wept and I wept. Tears that first fell as small as snowdrops bloomed into the size of peonies. They fell like a cloudburst. They fell like a flood. They became a flood. The flood overran the banks of the shallow mountain stream. The tears turned into waves, and the waves turned into a sea, this very sea on which we float, this very sea that you fell into—"

"Drowned in a vale of tears," mused Roger, repeating the phrase of Doveen the Serene.

Had he peered under her veil he would have seen the look of surprise on Princess Petulia's astonishingly beautiful face. "How did you know?"

"How did I know what?"

"I have decided to name this sea the Vale of Tears. I fished days and nights without end. I caught two hundred striped bass and fed them to the giant.

"For him it was a morsel, but the morsel cheered him. He could not rise, but he could talk. The most interesting talk I've ever had with a man! (Which isn't saying much, because all the others turned to stone.) What did we talk about? It's hard to say. He is not well educated, not educated at all. But because of his great height, he sees things. He observes. He misses very little. While I, behind my veil, miss everything. I learned much from the giant. Our talks dissolved my heart of stone.

"We talked all day, I fished at night. After a month, he was well enough to stand in the shallows. He took three or four steps and fell again into the sea. And that is where you found us. We have been floating for months. He seems near death and then he improves. I have saved his life over and over. From marauding pirates. From birds of prey. I fish, we talk. When he feels up to it, I ask him questions, and he tells me everything I want to know. More than once, he has made me smile behind my veil of tears as we drift on this Vale of Tears.

"One day, not long ago, a leaf fell into the sea nearby.

Why I noticed this leaf—or picked it out of the water—I have no idea. As you are surely aware, the leaf was Lady Sadie, my dear friend, my lady-in-waiting. She had blown for weeks in search of me. After two days she became herself again and we fell into each other's arms. She informed me of Prince Roger and his quest. Your quest. And that you would come to rescue me and lift my veil. And that you would *not* turn to stone. I was skeptical. But she was correct. I suppose I should look upon this as good news. And in a way, I do. My poor giant, Philip, has yet to see me without my veil. I'm afraid of what the shock might do to him. But on you"—she paused—"I have no effect whatsoever. I suppose the next step is that we return to the king, my father, collect your fortune, and wed." She spoke this last sentence in a whisper, as if she did not want the giant to hear.

"I don't make you laugh. You don't make me stone. I guess we're meant for each other," said Roger, without enthusiasm.

"Why should I laugh? Did you say something funny?" asked Princess Petulia.

"Lady Sadie's kidnapped?" said Roger, getting back to the person most on his mind.

"A week before you fell from the sky, a bandit appeared out of the sea. It was night. He caught us by surprise or we might have fought him off, as I have fought off pirates and marauders. He seemed to come from nowhere, giving me scarcely enough time to hide in the giant's shirt pocket.

Lady Sadie slipped on one of my veils and confronted him. I hated to have her face him alone, but I had a giant to protect. The man made no sense whatever. He seemed a little mad. He said that his best friend had done him wrong and he intended to get even with him by kidnapping the beautiful princess who was his quest. So he grabbed Lady Sadie and swam off with her."

Roger's face lost all color.

"You look ill," said Princess Petulia. "As if you might faint. I almost like you for the first time. You remind me of my giant."

"Where is she? I must rescue her!"

"I was under the impression that I was the one you were meant to rescue."

In response, Roger dove into the sea and swam for the only time in his life. First in one direction, then another. "Which way is shore?" he shouted at Princess Petulia.

She pointed south. "Shall I expect you back for my rescue . . . or not? I don't want to hurt your feelings, but it makes no difference to me!" she called after him.

Roger's voice came back from a quarter mile off. "Don't wait!"

Chapter 24

Tom Comes Back into the Book

Lady Sadie and Tom were having a conversation, one of many since he had kidnapped her. It was more or less the same talk.

Tom said something like: "I think we should leave today. Right now."

Lady Sadie would reply: "But what about Roger?"

Which prompted Tom to say: "I'm tired of waiting for Roger. If he was going to rescue you, he would have been here by now."

Usually these conversations took place after supper, each night by the dying embers of a fire. They were in a forest, but not the Forever Forest, thank heavens. This forest had many entrances and exits. And it was clear as day from one end to the other because the tallest trees weren't quite three feet high. For that reason, it was called the Short Forest.

Everything in the Short Forest was small-sized, from the trees to the flowers to the ponds (no bigger than bathtubs) to the paths (so narrow you had to walk sideways). And it was there that Tom had taken Lady Sadie (who he thought was Princess Petulia). He wanted Roger to find them fast, so he could get even fast.

Tom had cooked up his plot soon after Roger the Eagle dropped him off in the middle of the Dastardly Divide. "This is one more reason for me to get even," thought Tom, as he sat out two days and nights on an assortment of rocks. He wasn't angry enough to kill Roger. He was over that. But he *was* angry enough to defeat, mortify, and humiliate him so that his future would be bleak and his life in ruins. That struck Tom as the more mature approach, and just about as satisfying.

His plot was formed by the third day. He would destroy not Roger but his quest. As Roger had explained it, his quest was to rescue Princess Petulia. Tom would thwart that rescue by getting to her first. He didn't think it would be much of a problem. All he needed to do was walk out of the book and back in until he ran into her.

Luck was with him. On his fifth try, he found himself in the "Vale of Tears" chapter. The first thing he saw was a raft. Little did he know it was a giant! The second thing he saw was the veiled figure of Princess Petulia. Little did he know it was Lady Sadie! That's the way luck is sometimes. Even when it's on your side, it likes to kid around.

Now Lady Sadie was a most resourceful lady. She probably didn't have to be kidnapped if she didn't want to be. She let Tom kidnap her for two reasons. The first reason was to protect Princess Petulia, who was hiding in the giant's pocket. The second reason was that she was certain Roger would come to her rescue. And if Roger wasn't able to defeat Tom by himself, she was sure that she could help.

Lady Sadie didn't think much of Tom. Certainly the Roger she had begun to admire should have had better taste in friends. In her plainspoken way, she had come up with a word for Tom. The word was "Oaf."

How did they fill their week together, Tom and Lady Sadie? *She* filled it by teasing him. "Prince Roger is a mere boy, you are a full-grown man. Strong. Powerful."

"That's just what I was thinking," Tom replied.

"He is a prince on a quest. He believes that fortune is on his side. He will be overconfident and no match for a man such as yourself."

"It's amazing how two people from completely different backgrounds can think so much alike," said Tom.

"And after you have done what you will with him, you and I can go to the king, my father—"

"Why would I want to do that?" asked Tom.

"And I will remove my veil—"

"You're not serious!" exclaimed Tom.

"But he won't grant us permission to wed if I don't remove my veil."

Tom had never given a moment's thought to marrying Lady Sadie disguised as Princess Petulia. But now that she mentioned it . . . why not? "But—but—but won't I turn to stone?"

"But what if you don't?"

"But what if I do?"

"If you cared about me . . ." Lady Sadie turned away, pretending to be hurt.

Tom was fed up. "I don't care a fig about you, I just want to get even!"

"There is a way to find out if you'll turn to stone," said Lady Sadie.

"How?" said Tom, in a sulk.

"I will lift my veil just a smidgen, a tot . . ." She reached for her veil.

"No!" screamed Tom in terror. He hid his face behind his hands. "I'm not ready," he mumbled between his fingers.

"We'll do it tomorrow."

For seven days, that was the substance of their talks. And on the eighth day, Roger caught up with them.

Chapter 25
Stone

I know you want to hear if a terrible fight followed. It did. The results of that fight in a moment. But first I have to give you the conversation that preceded the fight. The way it was in those days, kings and princes and knights didn't go into battle without first engaging in a good long talk with their enemy. If you read Homer's book *The Iliad*, you'll find that his heroes, before entering battle, tell their opponents almost more about themselves than you'd want to tell your best friend. Where they're from, what their father does, their entire life's history, except, perhaps, what they did on their summer vacation.

Roger and Tom weren't called on to do that because they had been best friends before they became worst enemies. They already knew everything there was to know about each other. And that made it all the more difficult to find something to say. So they stood, dumbly exchanging stares by the glowing embers of the fire.

This was just after supper, when Tom and Lady Sadie were halfway through the same old conversation and he was in a terrible mood. So he was thrilled by Roger's interruption; he just wished one of them could find something to say.

Roger did, too. What he carried inside him was too confused to come out as words. What's more, he was exhausted after days of trekking—trek, trek, trek—through tall forests, middle-sized forests, and at long last the Short Forest. It troubled him that Tom could move with puzzling ease from place to place: out of the Forever Forest, out of the Dastardly Divide. Why was it easy for him and so hard for Roger?

This, Roger understood, was not a good subject for the conversation they were expected to have before the battle. He didn't want to start off a rescue sounding sorry for himself (like Tom), and besides, he was too hurt and confused to get personal. Tom surely wasn't his friend anymore, but he didn't feel like an enemy. So what was there to say except "I don't get it"? And that Roger was too proud to say in front of Lady Sadie. So he just waited by the fire, looking stupid.

It was clearly up to Tom to start the pre-battle conversation, if there was to be one.

"You're not an eagle anymore," Tom muttered.

"No," Roger said, relieved that someone had broken the ice.

"You're not a rock or a chair or a toad," Tom sneered.

"No."

"But I'm not laughing!" Tom looked proud in a mean sort of way.

"No."

"You're yourself. You're wearing your own body, which used to make me fall down laughing. But I'm not laughing. I'm not falling down. Ha-ha."

"You just laughed," Roger said, somewhat impatient with Tom's banter.

"Yes, but I'm not laughing with you, I'm laughing *at* you. So I'm getting even. Even before we start."

No doubt, Roger should have paid stricter attention to this nasty fellow with a sword, but his focus kept shifting to Lady Sadie behind the veil. "Are you all right, Lady Sadie?"

"I've been waiting for you to come and rescue me." She sounded pleased instead of irritated, and this made Roger's heart beat faster.

"Why are you calling her Lady Sadie?" Tom demanded to know.

Neither Roger nor Lady Sadie took the trouble to respond. "I'm glad you're safe," Roger said.

"I'm not safe yet," said Lady Sadie.

"No, but it's better than the Dastardly Divide, you've got to admit that."

"It's better. And it's worse," said Lady Sadie.

"Why do you say that?" Roger asked.

"We were alone on the Dastardly Divide. That was the good part." Her voice sounded husky behind the veil.

"We had some great times. Remember?" Roger's eyes glowed.

"I think about them day and night," murmured Lady Sadie.

Tom interrupted. "Aren't we supposed to duel or fight or something? I mean, what's going on here?"

Roger turned to look at Tom,

as if for the first time. "Were you ever really my friend?"

"I wasn't the one who deserted *you*," retorted Tom.

"You're right, I don't make you laugh anymore." He turned back to Lady Sadie. "Or you, either."

"You make me smile," she said.

"I don't see you smile." Roger frowned.

"I'm wearing a veil," Lady Sadie reminded him.

"Your eyes aren't smiling," Roger admonished.

"Forgive my plainspokenness, but we're standing here with a man who wants to kill you. I have no reason to smile."

Roger shook his head impatiently. "Nobody's going to kill anybody, that's your reason to smile."

"Then I will smile," said Lady Sadie.

Roger watched as her eyes, which were all he could see of her face, began to dance, then shimmer, then sparkle. Underneath the veil, he knew what he would find. He would find one of the world's great smiles, inspired by him! Not because he made people laugh—it wasn't that kind of smile. Roger sensed that. And sensing that, he too had to smile. So there they stood, Roger and Lady Sadie, not aware of anything else or anyone else (certainly not Tom!), only aware of their connecting smiles. Tom drew his sword and brandished it in the air. "You really tick me off. You make me feel as if I'm not here, after I went to a lot of trouble to get here."

"I never noticed your eyes before," said Roger, ignoring

Tom. "I mean, I noticed you *had* eyes, but I never noticed exactly what kind before."

As if in response, Lady Sadie's eyes widened enormously. "Look out behind you!" she shrieked.

Roger whirled to find Tom rushing at him, his sword aimed at Roger's right leg. "I can't stand being ignored!" roared Tom. "I'm going to get even by cutting off your right arm and your right leg so you go through the rest of your life off-balance!"

I said the fight was terrible, and it was. Terribly boring. The most boring fight you've ever read about in a story. If they make a movie out of this book, you can bet they'll shoot the fight to look exciting, but don't believe them. It wasn't that way at all. Tom was big and clumsy and, as much as he thought he wanted to maim Roger, his heart wasn't in it. He missed the easiest shots. He'd thrust his sword at Roger's arm, and though Roger neither ducked nor parried—in fact, he barely moved—the thrust was off by a mile.

Roger did so little to defend himself that it was hard to believe he was in a fight. Rather, it looked as if Tom was performing a solo sword dance and Roger was in the audience.

Lady Sadie was more excited than Roger, but after an hour of watching Tom charge wildly and miss, she concluded that the prince was perfectly safe, and that she had better things to do. She took herself off to a nearby minipond, partially hidden by a grove of short pines, and bathed for the first time in a week. As she bathed, she thought about Roger. Thinking about Roger made her hum to herself. The tune sounded happy.

Meanwhile, back at the fight, Roger tripped on a slippery patch of short weeds, more from fatigue than anything else. His sword flew from his hand and landed at Tom's feet. Roger sprawled on the ground, helpless. Tom saw that he had no choice but to kill him. It didn't matter that he didn't want to. He'd look bad if he didn't kill him.

He'd look soft, squeamish, babyish, weak, stupid, dumb.

By this time, Lady Sadie had finished bathing. As she donned the same dirty, smelly garments she had been wearing for days, her mood soured. Really, she'd had just about enough of this adventure! Feeling quite irritable now, she vaguely noticed Tom out of the corner of her eye raise his sword above his head, a mere second away from bringing it down on Roger's throat.

"Tom!" she called out sharply.

Tom whirled, relieved by the chance not to kill Roger.

Lady Sadie stepped out from behind the short pines. She approached Tom without a weapon, an argument, a plea for mercy, or a bid for pity. Helpless. Tom waited for her to think up something that would stop him from doing what he didn't really want to do.

During this extremely long pause, Roger had all the time in the world to leap to his feet and grab Tom in a headlock or hit him on the head with a rock or perform some act that would get him out of his tight spot.

But no, he just lay there, flat on his back, looking at the veiled figure of Lady Sadie, with the same stunned fascination that held Tom.

Lady Sadie took one step closer to Tom. He screamed. Even before she did it, he *knew*. Desperately, Tom threw his hands up to hide his face, completely forgetting that his right hand held a sword. The whack he gave himself staggered him. When the stars cleared, his first sight was of Lady Sadie loosening her veil. Tom feared that his heart would explode. Lady Sadie held her veil lightly between her thumb and forefinger. Tom turned white, his eyes bulged, his legs shook. Lady Sadie let the veil float off her fingers. It floated to the floor of the Short Forest. Behind the veil was revealed a perfectly average, pleasant-looking young woman. It made no difference. Tom turned to stone.

Chapter 26

Not Really

How could Tom turn to stone? Lady Sadie was certainly nice enough looking. More than nice: attractive. But attractive enough to turn a man into stone? I should say not.

No, Tom turned to stone because he had made up his mind that he was going to. Turning to stone was what happened to anyone who looked Princess Petulia in the face. Lady Sadie was passing for Princess Petulia. She tricked him. She dropped her veil, knowing it would terrify him. And that way, she could rescue Roger, who she seemed to rescue more times than not.

In fact, Tom didn't really turn to stone. But it took him a week of standing in one place, stiff as a statue, before he knew it. And that knowledge came only after he got thirsty and hungry. "Stone statues don't get thirsty" was his first thought. "Stone statues don't get hungry" was his second thought. "Stone statues don't think" was his third thought. And that's when he came to the conclusion—a week late, long after Roger and Lady Sadie had run off—that he was flesh and blood after all.

He didn't know how or why, all he knew was that he had changed from flesh and blood to stone—and back. No one could have convinced him otherwise. He was certain that, of all the suitors who Princess Petulia had made stone, only *he*, Tom, was special enough, was manly enough, to have what it takes to come back.

After he'd stuffed his stomach, Tom could think of nothing else but how extraordinary he was. How much better he must be than anyone else to make such an unprecedented comeback. Especially Roger. He didn't have to get even anymore. He *was* even. More than even. He could leave the book, not as a clown who fell into a patch of thorny roses, not as a fool left flat by his best friend, not as a buffoon or a bad guy—he could leave the book standing tall, a hero, the man who came back from stone.

Tom leaves the book now, never to return. I will write no more of him, other than to say that he lives happily ever after. All by himself. Waking every day to the cherished memory that once he was a statue and now he's not.

Chapter 27

The Next-to-Last Chapter

I've given this chapter that title because lots of times, when I'm near the end of a book I'm reading, I can't help but wonder how many more pages I have to go. So I flip to the end and peek. And find out things I didn't want to know. So for a long time I've thought that it would be a good thing for books to post distances the way they post mileage signs on highways.

Now back to our story. The first thing Princess Petulia said to Roger when he and Lady Sadie returned to Philip the giant raft was: "I know that you are the only man I have ever faced who did not turn to stone. I further know that you have made me your quest. Beyond that, I know that you expect to return to the king, my father, where you will receive your reward and we will be wed. I say this in a spirit of friendship, because in our brief time together I have come to know you as a good man with a kind soul."

"I am honored," said Roger, with a sinking heart.

"You are a true friend," said Princess Petulia.

"I am honored," said Roger, deeply depressed.

"True friend, I would rather die than marry you," said Princess Petulia.

"Whoopee!" shouted Roger, and he grabbed Lady Sadie and swung her in a circle in the air.

"I have fallen in love with the giant," said Princess Petulia.

"I have fallen in love with Lady Sadie!" shouted Roger.

And what did Lady Sadie have to say on this momentous occasion? She said to Roger: "As plain-thinking, plainspoken, and plain-looking as I am, I feel astonishingly beautiful when I am with you."

"Feed me," said the deepest, most rumbly voice Roger had ever heard. The giant was awake. Roger had forgotten he was there, except as someone to float on.

Roger, Lady Sadie, and Princess Petulia fished all night. They caught stripers, they caught mackerel, they caught flounder, they caught blues, and as they fished all night, they talked all night. The giant, too. After dining on three hundred fish, he was actually lively. So lively he picked a fight with Princess Petulia. A lovers' quarrel, their very first.

"I have fallen before, but not in love," he began. "This is my first time to fall in love. This is my last time. I have a request. It is the only request I will make of you in my lifetime. If you answer no, I will venture off . . . somewhere out of sight . . . where you will never see me again, however huge I am. But if you answer yes, I will love you and cherish you and serve you and never stray from your side till the day I die or you die or we die, which will never be, because we will be too happy. But only if you answer yes." The giant paused—and why not? He hadn't spoken this much in a long while.

"What is your request?" Princess Petulia asked during the pause.

The pause continued. The giant said nothing. After saying nothing for five minutes, he cleared his throat. The sound of his throat clearing caused nesting birds on shore to scatter. Fish fled to the bottom of the sea. "I would like," said the giant in his softest and humblest rumble of a voice, "for you to lift your veil."

"No," answered Princess Petulia. "You will turn to stone."

"I would like," repeated Philip the Giant in his softest and humblest voice, "for you to lift your veil."

"I dare not," answered Princess Petulia.

"Once I cared about your beauty. Then I might have turned to stone. Now I care about your love, your tenderness, your powers to heal, your fishing skills. You cannot change me into stone. You cannot change any man into stone. Not anymore. Because *you* are changed. I changed you before you could change me."

"How did you change me?" asked Princess Petulia in a trembling voice.

"Do you love me?" asked the giant, inhaling and exhaling so deeply that his breath sent the clouds scudding across the sky.

"From the bottom of my heart," answered Princess Petulia.

"Did you ever dream that you would love at all, much

less love from the bottom of your heart?" asked the giant with such resonating tenderness that the ripples stilled in the sea and the Vale of Tears shone like a mirror.

What could Princess Petulia do? She snatched off her veil and threw it into the Vale of Tears. She put her face up against the face of the floating giant and blissfully kissed him. Philip smiled. His smile was twice as long as Princess Petulia was tall. In his deep, rumbling voice, Philip said: "I have not turned to stone, I have turned to jelly."

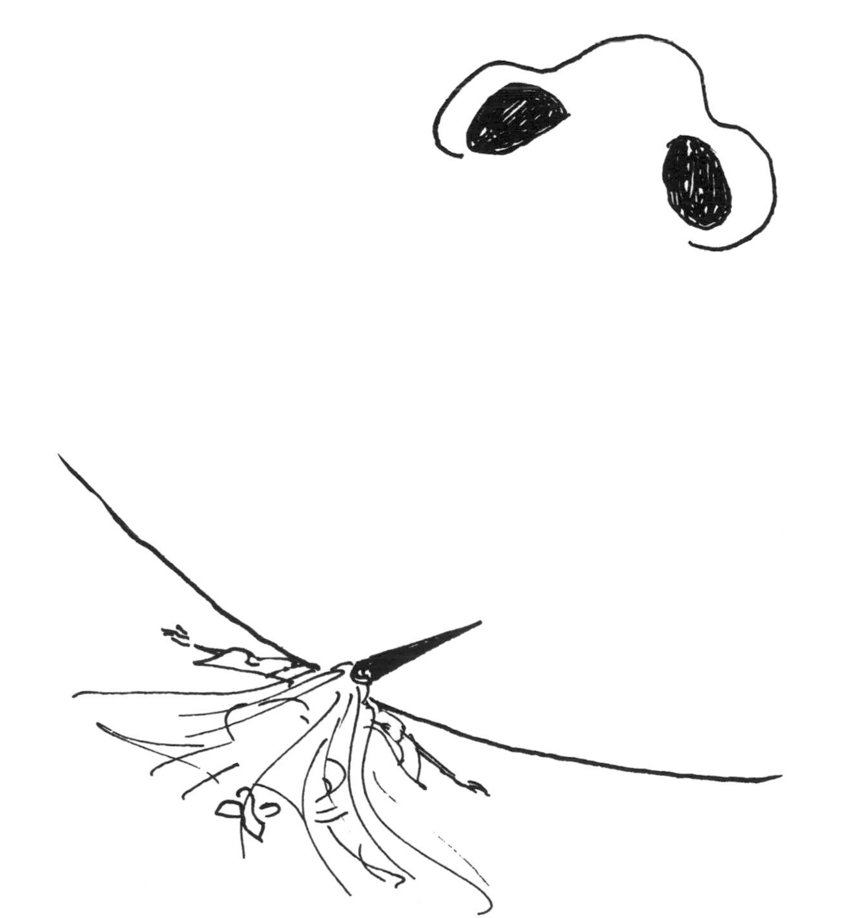

Chapter 28

Seven Pages to Go

True to Philip the Giant's prediction, no more men turned to stone at the sight of Princess Petulia's astonishingly, but no longer paralyzingly, beautiful face. And true to Tom's experience just before their fight, no one screamed with laughter at the sight of Roger anymore.

But first, the wedding. It was royal, it was double, it was performed by J. Wellington Wizard. The brides were given away by King Whatchamacallit. Roger and Sir Philip were each other's Best Man. Yes, he was Sir Philip now. Early on the morning of the royal wedding, King Whatchamacallit said "Kneel" to Philip the Giant, who had fully recovered from his long illness just in time to marry Princess Petulia. You may guess that "Kneel" was not the first word out of King Whatchamacallit's mouth. First, he said "Keel," then he said "Feel," then "Wheel," then "Deal," then "Surreal"—and *finally* he said "Kneel."

And Philip the Giant kneeled. This took half an hour. By the time he got his body folded in the several directions required in order for him to kneel, with his head down and his butt in the air, it was midafternoon and almost time for the wedding.

J. Wellington Wizard scanned the palace sundial anxiously, and muttered to the king, "Let's get on with it."

This didn't help matters. It served only to further confuse the king, who had intended to say, "Rise, Sir Philip the Tall," but said instead, "Skies, Tall Philip the Sir . . . Prize, Sir Tall the Philip . . . Rise, Sir Lies, Sir Pies in the Skies—er—Sir Sties in the Eyes . . ."

Finally, the job was done. Prince Roger and Sir Philip were wed to Princess Sadie (no longer Lady Sadie) and Princess Petulia. "Do you Princess Sadie and Princess

Petulia take Prince Roger and Sir Philip to be your royal wedded husbands, in sickness and health, for better or worse, in fights and forgiveness, in laughter and tears, now and forever, till death do you part?"

Now and forever takes years. This gave Roger lots of time to think. And one of the things he thought about he mentioned to Princess Sadie one day: "Dearest wife, what does it mean that I don't make anyone die laughing anymore?"

Princess Sadie considered the question for a while, and answered with her own question. "What does it mean that I'm not so plainspoken anymore?"

Roger looked surprised. "It's true. Sometimes you're plainspoken and sometimes you're soft-spoken and sometimes you yell and sometimes you purr."

To which Princess Sadie replied, "And sometimes you're so funny I want to hug and kiss you—and sometimes you're so sweet I want to hug and kiss you—and sometimes you're so sad I want to hug and kiss you—and sometimes you're so maddening I want to kick you."

Prince Roger scratched his head. "What does it all mean?"

"It means that if you go from the Forever Forest to the Dastardly Divide through the Valley of Vengeance over the Sea of Screams past the Mountain of Malice and nearly drown in the Vale of Tears, it is certain to have an effect on you."

Roger and Princess Sadie saw quite a bit of Princess Petulia and Sir Philip. The two royal couples built palaces side by side. Of course, Sir Philip's palace had to be taller

than three oaks sitting one atop the other. Once in a while, for old times' sake, the two couples went rafting on the Vale of Tears. Sir Philip was the raft. They fished, they talked, they sang songs, they laughed a lot. Often, it was Roger who made them laugh. Just as often, it was one of the others.

One day Princess Sadie suggested that they consider changing the name the Vale of Tears to the Lake of Love. Roger said, "Boy, are *you* not plainspoken anymore!" Everyone laughed so hard that the change of name was forgotten. In time, the name the Vale of Tears came to be regarded with great affection.

In their second year of marriage, Princess Sadie gave birth to a son they named Tom. At the christening, Roger ran into J. Wellington Wizard for the first time since the double wedding ceremony.

"Do you know that I nearly died on that quest of yours?" said Roger.

"The best thing that ever happened to you," said J. Wellington.

"Do you know that I nearly failed?" said Roger.

"You did fail," said J. Wellington. "The quest you went on was the wrong quest. Not that I had anything special in mind when I sent you, but by your third year in the Forever Forest the quest you were meant to go on was quite clear."

Roger could not believe his ears. "You mean I wasn't supposed to marry Princess Sadie?"

"You were supposed to marry Princess Daphne, who is not nearly as right for you," said J. Wellington. "All in all, I think you did brilliantly."

Roger went home and told Princess Sadie. Then he went across the street and told Princess Petulia and Sir Philip. Then he returned home and played with his baby son, Tom.

And what did he finally think of all this?

After a good deal of talk—with Princess Sadie, Princess Petulia, and Sir Philip—Roger decided that in his lifetime there might be a dozen, a hundred more quests, quests of all kinds waiting out there to be found. But where else would he have found this woman? Or this child? Or these friends?